PINE HILL MIDDLE SCHOOL
LIBRARY

KIDS and GUNS

The History, the Present, the Dangers, and the Remedies

By Ted Schwarz

PINE HILL MIDDLE SCHOOL LIBRARY

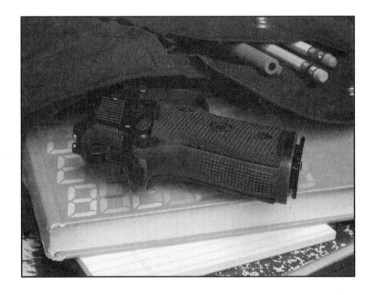

Franklin Watts
A Division of Grolier Publishing
New York   London   Hong Kong   Sydney
Danbury, Connecticut

Photographs ©:AP/Wide World Photos: 73 (Andrew Savulich); Archive Photos: 37 (Michael Carter), 68 (Fotos International), 10, 54 (Reuters/HO), 9 right (Reuters/John Sommers II); Center to Prevent Handgun Violence, Washington, DC.: 115, 119; Corbis-Bettmann: 13, 20; Gamma-Liaison, Inc.: 9 left (Steve Adams), 50 (Porter Gifford), 23, 45, 93 (Paul Howell), 6 (Rankin County News/Liat); Impact Visuals: 98 (Donna DeCesare), 61, 90 (Jerome Friar), 35 (Martin Jehnichen), 49 (Jonathan Kaplan), 113 (Carolina Kroon), 39 (Russ Marshall), 109 (Rick Reinhard), 64 (Martha Tabor); Monkmeyer Press: 102 (Paul Conklin), 70 (Rick Kopstein); North Wind Picture Archives: 33; PhotoEdit: 105 (Michael Newman); Photofest: 7, 58; Rothco Cartoons: 43 (by Boileau), 29 (by Dick Adair), 83 (by Wicks); Stock Boston: 107 (Bob Daemmrich), 86 (A. Ramey); Superstock, Inc.: 1.

Visit Franklin Watts on the Internet at:
http://publishing.grolier.com

Library of Congress Cataloging-in-Publication Data

Schwarz,Ted,
Kids and Guns: the history, the present, the dangers, and the remedies /
by Ted Schwarz.
p. cm.
Includes bibliographical references and index.
Summary: Examines the history of guns and gun use, issues of gun ownership and control, and the relationship between guns and violence involving young people.
ISBN 0-531-11723-5 (lib. bdg.)   0-531-16440-3 (pbk.)
1. Children and violence—United States—Juvenile literature. 2. Violence in children—United States—Juvenile literature. 3. Firearms ownership—United States—Juvenile literature. 4. Gun control—United States—Juvenile literature. [1. Gun control. 2. Violence.] I. Title.
HQ784.V55S38 1999
303.6'083—dc21   98-47197
                                                                            CIP
                                                                            AC

© 1999 by Ted Schwarz
All rights reserved. Published simultaneously in Canada.
Printed in the United States of America
4 5 6 7 8 9 10 R 08 07 06 05 04 03 02 01 00

CONTENTS

When Guns Come to School

Luke Woodham is one of the teenagers whose violence recently made headlines on television and in news magazines. A sixteen-year-old high school sophomore in Pearl, Mississippi, he was the fat kid with glasses found in every school. He was the last to be chosen for pickup ball games, the kid pointedly not invited to birthday parties, a good student but not one to get involved with any of the clubs. He got lucky only once, when he asked Christina Menefee for a date and she accepted. Christina was pretty, smart, athletic, outgoing, and popular enough to be a prom queen. She saw something in Luke none of the other kids saw, and she found she enjoyed his company.

She enjoyed it, that is, until Luke's mother insisted on coming along on their early dates; until the other kids started teasing her about her new boyfriend; until the stress of dating Luke outweighed the pleasure of his friendship.

That was when Christina gently told him they should start seeing others. There was no one else in her life. There was nothing wrong with Luke. It was just time for both of them to be open to other relationships.

Christina's parents thought she had let him down easy. They thought she had been gentle and honest. Luke thought otherwise. Luke went home and got a gun.[1]

Luke Woodham, in custody in Pearl, Mississippi

For fifty years, movies and television shows have portrayed teen violence as something found only in the inner city. When your grandparents went to the movies after World War II, violent teens were shown as, in the terms of those days, poor white trash. The boys rode motorcycles or drove hot rods—customized cars with high-powered engines—and they drank beer, the most outrageous signs of rebellion imaginable in those more innocent times. The girls in the movies noisily chewed gum in school, sassed their elders, rode on the backs of the motorcycles, and sometimes had sex before marriage. They were shown as mindless Barbie dolls in tight clothes, urging their boyfriends to fight each other, sometimes fighting among themselves, especially if they went to jail where, in the movies of the 1950s, it seemed everyone was beaten or raped. The graphic action usually took place off camera, but there was no question as to what had happened.

The stories sound silly today. They were low-budget morality tales for nice suburban kids, showing what could happen to them if they ever acted like less fortunate teens. The latter were the ones born into blue-collar families living in all-white, low-income neighborhoods. These films were frequently shown in drive-in theaters, often paired with other low-budget features of equally "adult" themes.

In more recent years the movie villains live in the same bad neighborhoods, but instead of being white, they are usually either black or Hispanic. The victims of their violence are usually one another, though occasionally they attack a nice, white, suburban teen or adult who ventures into the "jungle" that is the inner city—at least in the movies.

Teen Age Crime Wave, *a typical movie of the 1950s*

Luke Woodham would never have been cast as the villain in a movie about teens in crisis. He was a white kid raised in Pearl, Mississippi, the type of suburban community that is the American dream for many adults. Churches dominate almost every corner, much as convenience stores, small hair salons, and neighborhood bars are found in less desirable locations. The variety of ways to worship indicate that no one approach to theology dominates the community of approximately 22,000 people.

Unemployment is low in Pearl, and no obviously homeless people are visible. Many of the homes are small and relatively inexpensive; old and rusting cars and trucks sit in some of their driveways. Local socializing takes place in coffee shops and churches. And the local high school is the center of much of the community life. The football stadium holds 12,000 people and is regularly filled. The high school choir travels extensively to perform, and the high school band is equally respected. The high school building is in a dense wooded area midway along a road that winds almost a mile through the school's grounds. The educational program is so good that the school is often rated among the top ten public high schools in the nation.

There were no metal detectors in Pearl High School on October 1, 1997, when Luke Woodham left home. There were no security guards at the school; no sinister characters hanging around outside, whispering about drugs to susceptible students. Pearl was the kind of community where parents have long trusted the educational system to help their children reach their full potential. It was the kind of community where parents know their children are safe when attending classes or participating in after-school programs.

Or so they thought until Luke Woodham got a gun, went to school, and started shooting at his classmates.

The tranquil suburban setting of Heath High School in Paducah, Kentucky, where three students were killed and five others were injured; fourteen-year-old Michael Carneal(right) was charged with the attack.

Parents of students attending Heath High School in Paducah, Kentucky, were equally comfortable about their children's safety. Located along the Ohio and Tennessee rivers, the city and its people have a reputation for friendliness and hospitality. They also take their religion seriously, the school allowing an informal prayer meeting and Bible fellowship each morning in the entrance hall. Those meetings, led by Ben Strong, a popular football player whose father is an Assembly of God minister, reflected the serious nature of many of the students. They had little reason to expect a schoolyard shooting. Then, on December 1, 1997, Michael Carneal, a fourteen-year-old freshman, came to school with his backpack, a pistol, two shotguns, two rifles, and seven hundred rounds of ammunition. When he stopped firing, three classmates were dead and several others were wounded.[2]

It is not just high school students who have made headlines by bringing guns to school and shooting their classmates. Andrew "Drew" Golden was eleven years old and a student at Westside Elementary School in Jonesboro, Arkansas, when he sneaked into school, pulled the fire alarm, then ran outside to join his friend Mitchell Johnson, age thirteen. They hid among some nearby trees with three rifles and seven handguns. It was an area they knew well, an area where most of the children would routinely go during a fire drill.

The time was 12:35 P.M. on March 24, 1998. It was fifth period, and many of the students suspected the alarm was a prank. Perhaps someone was trying to avoid a test or was playing a joke. Routine drills were usually expected by the staff, and they seemed surprised to hear the alarm. Still, everyone followed the standard procedure, making quick, orderly exits from the school.

Mitchell Johnson (left) and his cousin, Andrew Golden, were charged with the Jonesboro school shooting.

Suddenly there was the sound of gunfire. Wounded children began falling to the ground. Brittheny Varner, eleven, was struck. Paige Ann Herring, twelve. Natalie Brooks, twelve. Child after child until nine children and one teacher lay wounded, four other children and one other teacher, Shannon Wright, lay dead. Twenty-two rounds of ammunition had been fired in four minutes by Drew and Mitch. Hundreds of lives were changed forever.[3]

Kids and guns. The combination is terrifying for students everywhere around the country. Some schools have installed metal detectors and hired security guards, daily reminders that trouble could occur at any moment, that elsewhere, children and teenagers have taken the lives of their classmates. Many schools ignore the issue, trusting that it can't happen in their facilities. But how great is the danger? Why is it happening? And what can you do if a friend or classmate starts talking about violence?

Chapter *2*
Guns in History

When the earliest settlers brought guns to America, they considered them tools, little different from hammers or axes. The weapons were crude, allowing the firing of a single shot. Reloading took almost a minute. Gunpowder had to be poured into the weapon, and then a metal ball tamped in place. The trigger sent the hammer against a piece of flint, setting a spark that ignited the gunpowder, explosively propelling the metal ball through the barrel of the rifle or handgun. The force was great enough to kill wild animals, both for food and for protection, if the shooter was fairly close. The guns were extremely inaccurate, but they were better than the Native Americans' bows and arrows that had to be used at dangerously close range. A colonist with a rifle could shoot a buffalo from enough distance to be able to run away or climb a tree if the shot missed and the animal charged. A Native American using a bow and arrow had to ride a horse alongside the buffalo in order for the arrow to have enough force to penetrate the thick hide. This made for greater chances of injury or accidental death, especially if the horse fell during the encounter with the frightened buffalo.

Handguns and long guns (rifles) were used in warfare, but not as such weapons are used today. Instead,

A soldier of 1776 fills a musket from a powder horn.

they were used to make noise and smoke to create panic and confuse the enemy. Sometimes the balls struck their marks. Most times they didn't. Both sides in a battle learned that a volley of rifle fire had to be followed by a rush against the enemy. Then the real killing started with bayonets. In fact, most battles were fought at such close range that the shooters did not have time to reload for a second shot before the enemy was upon them for hand-to-hand combat.[1]

These were the weapons the Founders knew when writing the Constitution. These were the weapons that had caused Ben Franklin, a patriot leader in the Revolutionary War, to suggest that the colonists arm themselves with bows and arrows and stage sneak attacks on the British encampments.

When guns were improved, most of the changes made them better weapons of war. The bullet replaced powder and shot. The revolver replaced the single-barreled handgun. The repeating rifle became popular, especially after ways were found to make it more accurate at ever greater distances.

Television programs and movies about the Old West often show all the men in a town wearing revolvers in holsters strapped around their waists. Sometimes there is a dramatic handgun showdown on Main Street. Sometimes there are battles between cowboys and cattle rustlers, or stagecoach guards and pursuing bandits. Violence is a constant companion, and the handgun rules the West—at least in the movies.

Reality was less violent. There were occasional gunfights, though they were rarely quick-draw contests with the man who gets his handgun from his holster the fastest winning. Most men did not carry handguns because they were not as practical as other weapons. Rifles and shotguns put food on the table and kept coyotes away from their livestock. Lawmen and hunters preferred their accuracy.

Handguns were carried by lawmen, as they sometimes needed a weapon in close quarters. Still, handguns were not the preferred weapon for fighting. In fact, when teenage and adult outlaws had handguns, the weapons often proved to be their own worst enemies.

For example, Jesse James was seventeen and serving as a Confederate guerrilla during the Civil War when he gained a reputation as a crack shot with a handgun.[2] Yet neither the weapon nor the user were very good. He shot off the tip of his own finger while cleaning a revolver. And during one bank robbery, when he tried to kill an unarmed bank teller, he fired off six rounds at close range—and missed with every shot.

The image of the tough, dangerous gunfighter stems mostly from publicity generated by fiction writers and

14

lies told by the gunfighters themselves. Bat Masterson, who was both an outlaw and a law enforcement officer at various times in his early career, was said to have killed thirty-one men in 1884 alone. The handgun was his constant companion, and he used it with skill—or so the myth suggested.

In truth, the only time Masterson killed anyone was when he was seriously wounded and had to fire in self-defense. He found the handgun more effective as a club for beating prisoners when he administered his own form of brutal "justice" against the accused. Later he became a sportswriter in New York and occasionally supplemented his income by selling his notched gun from his days as a lawman. Each notch represented a person killed, or this was his claim. The fact that he bought a supply of guns specifically to notch, and that they had no part in his past, was his secret.[3]

Cowboys working the range carried sidearms because they could be used for killing snakes, destroying badly injured livestock, and turning aside cattle stampedes. They were not, as movies show, for protection against outlaws and cattle rustlers. In fact, they were considered of such limited use that they were rarely well maintained. The cowboy regularly used the revolver as a hammer, something that would never happen with a weapon necessary for self-defense.

When dealing with criminals stealing livestock, the cowboys favored such weapons as the Winchester repeating rifle, which came in a variety of types. Its lever action allowed rapid repeat fire, and its long barrel assured accuracy. Winchesters could be used for hunting, and they could be used in areas where Indian raids occasionally occurred. The first Winchester was sold in 1866, and though it was designed for civilian use on ranches and elsewhere, it also became popular with soldiers.

As an example of how handguns were sometimes used, there are accounts of Wild Bill Hickock, a notorious lawman of the Old West, using his revolvers to kill stray dogs. There was no animal protective league back then. Stray dogs were nuisances that often killed livestock. So great was the problem of strays that lawmen like Wild Bill Hickock supplemented their pay by killing the wild dogs for a twenty-five cents per dog bonus.[4]

Hickock's death came as the result of a handgun, though again, not as in the movies. He was playing cards in a saloon when an enemy sneaked up and shot him in the back. This was not surprising because the saloons and gambling halls were violent places. In fact, manufacturers designed guns for use in such locations. Among these were deringers and pepperbox guns, which fired four bullets in rotation.

The pepperbox had four very short barrels. Sometimes the barrels rotated as the gun was fired, a little like a squared-off revolver, although the barrels, not just the bullet cylinder, revolved with each shot. Other pepperbox handguns had stationary short barrels and a revolving firing pin that struck each barrel in turn.

The four-inch deringers usually fired one shot and were meant for close-in shooting of humans. The original and the imitations (usually called derringers, an extra r added to the name) were only effective at close range.[5]

Even in areas where settlers faced violence from their neighbors, handguns were not used for protection because they were both inaccurate and expensive. The original Samuel Colt revolver sold for thirty-five dollars at a time when many workers earned only a dollar a day. This made the market so limited that the original Colt factory closed after six years.[6]

What brought the handgun back was a series of wars. The United States fought Mexico in 1846. Fourteen years later, the Civil War began. We sent soldiers to fight in the Spanish-American War, World War I, World War II, Korea, Vietnam, and so on. Most of the killing was at a long distance, but when fighting was close-in, the revolver was desirable. Just as the rifle was a tool for survival for settlers, so the handgun became a tool for killing people in wartime.

For families settling the West, a rifle was the tool of choice for getting meat for the dinner table or for stopping a predator endangering livestock or, occasionally, children. Men, women, and children all knew how to handle rifles and shotguns so they could kill wild turkeys, deer, buffalo, rabbits, and squirrels. The guns could bring down ducks, geese, and other birds. The more rural the settlement, the more uses a family could find for the animals they shot. Animal hides were used for shoes, clothes, bedding, and hats. A large deer or buffalo was a one-stop shop for food and clothing.

Even in some urban areas, kids understood this use of the gun, and not just in the nineteenth century. During the 1930s, the era of the Great Depression, children would shoot or trap muskrats along lakes and rivers. After the animal was killed, the skin was removed, stretched, and dried. Then the hide was sold to an independent shop that made it into clothing, or to a chain department store that shipped it to a manufacturing plant. Adults and children earned as much as $3.00 for each muskrat properly prepared.

"We had a business," said Lou Egerer, a retired attorney who, as a young teenager, during the Depression, hunted and trapped for food. "I went out at 3 A.M. every morning, setting my traps and checking them to see what I caught. I worked until 7 A.M., then

PINE HILL MIDDLE SCHOOL LIBRARY

went home with whatever I had caught. While I ate breakfast and got ready for school, my younger brother skinned the animals and hung the furs on stretchers in our garage. He'd put the meat in salt water to draw out the blood. Our father sold the meat to the butcher for 25 cents, the poor furs to Sears for $2.25 each, and the better furs to a trapper who paid $2.75 each for quality. We would have 10 to 15 a day at least.

"Muskrats look like rabbits, only stumpier. It was cheap meat. The butcher sold each animal for 50 cents, double what he paid us. I averaged about 1,500 pelts every year, making more money than many grown men."

The shotgun and rifle were tools for children like Lou Egerer. Hunting and fishing helped feed the family or brought in cash. "It never occurred to us to shoot anybody. Guns were not for settling arguments. When we got mad, we used our fists," said Egerer.[7]

Retired accountant and former circus performer Chauncey Holt was raised in Appalachia during the era of Prohibition. Appalachia was among the poorest regions in the United States. Communities were isolated, and jobs were scarce. Few people owned luxuries such as cars. But everyone owned a shotgun or rifle for hunting, and many kids carried rifles to school so they could shoot game on their way home. "It was like having an after-school job," Holt explained.[8] Instead of after-school jobs, Appalachian kids helped their families by hunting. And because hunting laws were not always strictly enforced in rural America, no one considered whether it was hunting season. If meat was needed for food or to barter for clothing or something else, the kids would put down their books at the end of classes, pick up their guns, and take care of business.

Even today, in many parts of the country, families own guns as tools for hunting, enabling them to live better than they otherwise could. In Arizona, for example, perhaps as much as 80 percent of the land is either Native American reservations or protected wilderness. In some areas, wild animals abound, and during hunting season families sometimes shoot enough meat to last six months. Pickup trucks often have rifle racks mounted in the rear windows, and some people go to work with a rifle or shotgun in the rack. They may be bankers, doctors, lawyers, construction workers, or ranch laborers. The truck may be battered, rusted, and filthy, or an expensive new sport utility vehicle, fully equipped with cell phone and CD player. But the rack is still likely to be in place, the owner likely to be in the woods whenever it is legal to shoot deer, javelina (wild boar), or wild turkey.

Handguns in such areas are viewed differently than they are in the East and Midwest. Most people living in urban areas look upon handguns as weapons of protection against criminals. Certainly the handgun has never been seen as a tool, like a rifle or shotgun. It is far less accurate over long distances. Handguns are carried in areas where bears, mountain lions, and similar predators live. Workers in isolated areas where some wild animals look upon them as a potential lunch have found that it is a good idea to carry a long-barreled handgun in a holster for use in an emergency.

Wild game hunters in areas with poisonous snakes frequently carry handguns loaded with "snake shot." This is a bullet that shoots several pellets, like a shotgun. If a snake is about to strike, the handgun is used to kill it. Since the threatened hunter is probably scared and shaking and likely to miss with an ordinary bullet, the multiple pellets of the snake shot assure the snake is killed before it can bite. And, unlike bullets which can kill for a distance of a mile or more, the

Billy the Kid, seen shooting a shopkeeper in an early engraving

snake shot is deadly for only about fifteen feet. Beyond that it is only slightly more dangerous than a high-powered BB gun. Again, these weapons are tools.

Protection against wild animals is one reason even some city dwellers keep a rifle or shotgun. Areas in and around Beverly Hills, that glamorous playground of the rich and famous, have coyotes that have lost their fear of humans. When hungry, they move into residential areas where they have been known to attack household pets and even small children. These are not country cabins surrounded by wilderness. These are often lavish estates close to major highways. But enough land exists in its natural state to allow some coyotes to survive, along with their prey. Although coyotes don't often wander into the movie colony, the threat of their occasional appearance leads some homeowners to keep .22 caliber rifles or low-powered shotguns on hand to scare them away.

The fact that guns were tools during the frontier period and the Depression years did not stop some kids from using them for illegal purposes. Teenager William Bonney was one of the most notorious outlaws in the nation when he terrorized the West as Billy the Kid. The major difference between his actions and those of someone such as Luke Woodham was that Billy was using his gun to steal money; his violence was related to his robberies. Luke wanted to see his classmates die.

The difference between the kids who turned to illegal activity in the nineteenth and early twentieth centuries and violent kids today is that past violence rarely occurred in schools. Kids then went into small towns and big cities, becoming robbers or hired "muscle," using their guns to extort or to intimidate. During the Prohibition era, crime paid, and sometimes very well. Lives were frequently cut short in disputes over bootleg territory, illegal nightclubs, and gang wars. But the violence was mostly for disputes between bad guys, and the majority of the victims were rival criminals.

So why do kids seem to be more violent today? Why are guns increasingly found in schools? What risks do you face when you go to your classes each day?

Chapter 3

The Scope of the Problem

There are an estimated 192 million guns privately owned in the United States today. These range from single-shot weapons to fully automatic weapons capable of shooting hundreds of rounds a minute. They are found in urban ghettos and in the mansions of millionaires. An estimated 500,000 guns are stolen each year, 80 percent—four out of every five—taken from private homes. The remainder are stolen from military armories and gun shops.[1]

In television programs and movies, handguns seem a part of inner-city gang life. Sometimes it appears that every gang member has a small arsenal of weapons. Yet in truth, guns are more likely to be found in the homes of ordinary people, individuals who feel the need for self-protection. Sometimes these people fear street crime. Sometimes they or someone close to them has been the victim of street crime. Sometimes they believe that some secret faction of government is endangering their rights. They claim that owning a gun is the first line of defense against such tyranny.

Some of the handguns kept in homes are souvenirs from past wars. Men who fought in World War II sometimes retained their .45-caliber automatic sidearms. Many of the guns were so unreliable that the soldiers

A variety of handguns

kept the ammunition clip out of the guns when carrying them. They loaded the weapon only if they found themselves in a combat situation. The rest of the time they feared the gun accidentally going off more than they feared the unseen enemy. Still they brought the guns home from the war, lethal souvenirs that were sometimes kept in a bedside table, sometimes mounted on the wall, sometimes put away and forgotten over the years.

Guns for Protection

The type of gun purchased for home protection varies with the fears, fantasies, and knowledge of the gun buyer. Some people like the idea of owning a high-powered handgun for home protection. They buy a .357-magnum revolver or a .44-caliber handgun, unaware of how dangerous these weapons are. (The higher the caliber number, the larger and more powerful the bullet. Target shooting rifles, which can also be used for small game, are often .22-caliber. Police weapons are usually .38-caliber or the more powerful .357-magnum, which fits the same size handgun but requires a sturdier barrel. The .44-caliber and .45-caliber weapons are the most powerful handguns available.) These weapons are capable of firing bullets that can go through the engine block of a car. If a person fires one at home and hits an intruder, the bullet may pass through the intruder, go through the wall and across the street, and strike an innocent neighbor with killing force. If one is fired in an apartment building, the bullet may go through one wall after another, striking anyone who has the misfortune to be in its path.

Smaller caliber weapons fire less powerful ammunition, which is safer since if the target is missed, the bullet can be stopped more easily. A .22-caliber bullet fired inside a house will probably be stopped by the wall. A more powerful handgun can send the bullet through the wall onto the street where a passerby may be hit. This is why .22 caliber is a popular size for target shooting. It is also the type of weapon—usually a .22-caliber rifle—that many parents give their young children to introduce them to shooting.

Yet even with the less dangerous .22-caliber rifle or handgun, the bullet may travel 1 to 1.5 miles before stopping. Both .22-caliber revolvers and automatics are popular for assassinations by organized hit men.

Fear and Guns

Some people feel that guns make the nation secure. They cite the "right to bear arms" provided for in the Second Amendment of the Constitution (see Chapter 4). They believe that citizens need to be armed to prevent a tyrant from taking control of the nation. Other guns are bought not so much because the owner wants to protect his or her home but because of a fear of the streets. These individuals carry a gun in a pocket or purse, a briefcase, or a car. They fear that they will one day be the victim of a violent criminal and want to protect themselves. The fact that in some places it is illegal to carry a concealed handgun does not prevent them from having one.

A few years ago in New York City, a city that has severe penalties for carrying a concealed handgun, a man named Bernard Goetz took a handgun on the subway. He had been robbed in the past and was terrified of being attacked again. When four youths acted in a manner he felt was menacing, he drew his handgun and fired at them. Goetz's highly publicized story made some people fear that the subway was dangerous, even though crime statistics indicated that robberies on the subway were highly unusual. Later, Goetz was charged with failing to have a license for the gun he carried, illegally hidden on his body. He was also sued in civil court by one of the youths who claimed to be paralyzed as a result of the shooting.

Studies conducted at retirement communities such as Sun City, Arizona, and St. Petersburg, Florida, have found that the more active people are outside their homes, the less they feel the need for a handgun. Shutins and television watchers who spend their evenings at home are more likely to own guns and to believe the streets are unsafe. Older adults who participate in social clubs, volunteer work, bowling leagues, and other activities that take them out in the evening are more likely to feel the streets are safe. They are less likely to own a weapon. It is hard to say whether more fearful people choose to stay in, or whether getting out shows people the world is not filled with danger at every step.

But it does seem that fear increases with withdrawal from the world.

Other studies have been concerned with the impact of the media on society. The findings are always similar. Television programs often portray violence. This is true in police shows, in hospital and courtroom dramas, and in many soap operas. News-program directors regularly choose the most violent story for the lead, giving it an importance it may not have. Local news directors frequently follow the maxim "If it bleeds, it leads." They believe that people are fascinated by violence, and they either ignore or don't care that the audience will think that the news story that opens a program is the most important.

What does this mean? Suppose your city's mayor announces that a major manufacturing plant is being built in your community. There will be hundreds of new jobs, work your family and your friends' families desperately need. And suppose on the same day a news photographer happens to arrive at a bar where two drunk friends showing off their newly purchased handguns accidentally shoot each other. Neither is badly hurt, but the videotape shows them in pain, with paramedics rushing to provide first aid, their uniforms blood-stained as they work. The business announcement, which may mean millions of dollars for the city, is made by the mayor, the company president, and the president of the local chamber of commerce on the site of the new construction. The image is "talking heads," without the intensity of the shooting. Which do you think will be the lead story, the one meant to grab you and keep you from changing the channel? And, unfortunately, which impression is left: that the city is a violent place, or that the economic future is promising?

Some people work at jobs that require them to be in areas or situations where they do not feel safe. Late-night workers who must use public transportation frequently fear that they are targets for criminals. A woman who travels home after dark, and waits at a bus stop on a deserted street, may feel that anyone could drive up and attack her. Since kidnappings and rapes have occurred in these circumstances, she may feel justified in carrying a handgun in her purse or pocket.

Delivery-truck drivers who have to go anywhere a package has been sent sometimes feel they need to be armed. Jim Radcliff, a Cleveland man who started a package delivery business, always carried a .32-caliber revolver in his jacket pocket. "I used to go into high-crime areas where many people were unemployed. You could see drug deals on some corners. I figured I might be a target since I carried things you could sell on the streets. One day as I was making my deliveries, I stopped at a stop light. Suddenly the back door of my van was opened and a guy started climbing inside. I pulled out my gun, pointed it at him, and told him I'd shoot him if he didn't get out. He took off running."

Jim admits that he could have prevented the incident. "All I had to do was keep the van doors locked, except when loading or unloading a package. The guy took a chance of trying the door handle and was probably as startled to find the door opened as I was to find him climbing into the van. I don't think he wanted to hurt me. I think he wanted to grab something and run. I almost killed him, and all because I was relying on my gun and not on the common sense of locking the van doors."

Jim began locking his van doors but still carried his gun. In the three years he continued his business, that was the only time he ever had a problem.

In Milwaukee, Wisconsin, store-manager John Hwika bought a .45-caliber automatic handgun for protecting his home. He was showing his mother how to load, unload, and use the safety catch on the weapon when his pet poodle, Benji, lovingly leaped on Hwika's chest, causing the gun to go off. The bullet struck him in the chest. He lived long enough only to reach for the telephone in an effort to dial 9-1-1.

The reasons people buy guns to keep in their homes or to carry when they are traveling to and from work are as varied as the owners. Most of the people who own handguns are not criminals. Most of the handgun owners consider themselves responsible people. Yet what matters to you is that handguns are everywhere. Whether you live in the city, the suburbs, or the country, if your family does not have a handgun, chances are that someone close to you will own one. It is this easy access that adds to the problems they can cause.

The Accidental Victims

Gun violence is not just about one person shooting another. Many victims are people the shooters never intended to hurt. For example, when gang rivalry heats up, gangs sometimes may try to ambush a rival gang member. They may know that the person is going to attend an outdoor event on a certain street. One gang member drives a car past while another leans out the window with a gun. As the car passes the intended victim, the shooter fires off round after round of ammunition, trying to hit the target. Sometimes the bullets go where expected. Other times they strike passersby, people sleeping in nearby apartments or houses, and others. The bullet does not have a brain. It travels rapidly in a straight line wherever the barrel was

pointed when the trigger was pulled. It can kill for a distance of well over a mile. And if a drive-by shooting takes place in a densely populated area, every bullet will probably strike someone.

Drive-by shootings may leave one or more people dead, or wounded. For the wounded, this can mean anything from a few days in the hospital to a lifetime in a wheelchair. Unintended victims of bullets have had their spinal cords severed, have been left incontinent, have been blinded. Some have been left with brain damage. All have experienced extreme pain, sometimes resulting in addiction to painkillers, years of repeated surgery, or other problems.

One bullet can change a life forever. A student who planned to dance the night away at the senior prom attends in a wheelchair, if at all. A student who planned to be a surgeon may have to fight to get into medical school and then must settle for a specialty that can be handled with physical limitations. An athlete who counted on an athletic scholarship fails to get one because he or she can no longer perform on the field. And a student who was a leader may need help getting dressed, eating, and using the toilet.

Chapter 4
The Right to Own Guns

Why Americans have the right to own guns is a hotly debated question. The Second Amendment to the Constitution states: "A well regulated Militia being necessary to the security of a free State, the right of the people to keep and bear arms shall not be infringed." But what does this mean?

The Well Regulated Militia

At the time of the writing of the Constitution, toward the end of the eighteenth century, a militia was the equivalent of today's National Guard, and the arms in question were smoothbore flintlock muskets. They were extremely inaccurate, perhaps good for a hundred yards in the hands of a skilled shooter. They were also so difficult to reload, taking almost a minute of work between shots, that a shooter was likely to be killed in hand-to-hand combat before the musket could be fired twice. A battle was often decided when one side fired their rifles and then was overwhelmed by the other side charging them with bayonets while they reloaded.

The musket was a tool of the militia. The militia was composed of all the people in a community. Advocates of a militia believed it assured both liberty and security. The other option for protection was a

31

standing army, which people feared because they had just fought Britain's standing army in the Revolutionary War.

What is seldom discussed today are the debates about the Second Amendment that took place during the Continental Congress. Militias required universal service, and some of the Founders worried that such universal service could lead to the country's entire population being forced to live under military discipline. Others feared that Congress would pass a law allowing it to create its own elite militia, in effect a standing army. A Virginia delegate to the Congress, Richard Henry Lee, stated that he felt that such an elite army might be used against the citizens.

Alexander Hamilton was an artillery officer in the Revolutionary War. His position was that militia fighters were never as good as regular troops. James Madison feared that if one state controlled a militia, there could be a danger to other states. He suggested organizing a militia under national authority and having an elite militia to handle problems where greater training and discipline were necessary. Madison felt that ideally every white male would be part of the militia so they could act against excesses of the national government and the regular army.

These arguments about the militia show how much the Revolutionary War was influencing the delegates' thinking. They were dealing with issues relating to England and the king's army which had been used to try to stop them from gaining independence. Fear of a national government was still strong for many. There was great concern that they do whatever was necessary to protect their hard-won freedom.

Another argument advanced during the debate over the Second Amendment was that if Congress could arm

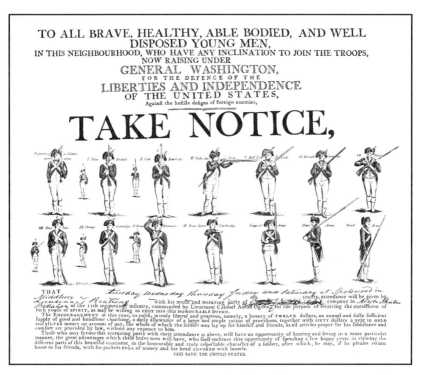

This recruiting poster, to raise the first American army for the Revolution, shows soldiers drilling.

citizens, it could also disarm them. The amendment's final wording was intended to protect the right to keep and bear arms.

A year after the passage of the Second Amendment and the Bill of Rights, the debate still continued. The Uniform Militia Act was proposed in 1792. It would have forced all able-bodied white males between the ages of eighteen and forty-five to be enrolled in the militia. Each male would have had to arm himself with either a musket or firelock (a variation of the musket with a slightly different firing mechanism), a bayonet, and ammunition.

While the dismissal of women was standard in those days, the racial discrimination was unusual—

despite the fact that the Constitution recognized the institution of slavery. Free blacks frequently served in militias. However, some of the act's supporters believed that a time might come when a militia would be called upon to put down a slave revolt. They did not believe free blacks would be willing participants in such a call to duty.

Gun Control Advocates

People who are against gun ownership feel that the militia is not needed. The National Guard, which can be called into service at the request of a state's governor and can also be called to active duty with the U.S. military, acts as a militia.

A somewhat different form of militia has appeared in some states, where citizens' groups have declared themselves militias, insisting that they have the right to arm themselves with whatever sophisticated weapons they can afford. But they are not acting under the authorization of their state's government. And in some instances they break laws, claiming that the U.S. government imposes illegal taxes and that they have the right to issue their own form of money. Some are separatist groups, claiming patriotism by calling themselves a militia, yet committing crimes that make them outlaws.

Gun ownership opponents believe that the Constitution does not provide for the ownership of guns for personal protection. Further, they argue that it does not specify the type of weapon someone can own, although the 1792 act did mention muskets. For this reason, the opponents of gun ownership challenge those people who say the Constitution gives them the right to own any weapon they desire without federal interference.

The National Rifle Association seeks new members at a gun show.

The United States Supreme Court, the body that ultimately determines which laws are constitutional and which are not, has never ruled that Americans cannot have guns. However, it has said that it is constitutional for a city or state to limit gun ownership. Such limitations include New York's tough Sullivan Law, which requires special licensing of handguns, and federal law H.R. 1025, commonly called the Brady Bill.

The Brady Bill

James Brady was partially paralyzed after he was shot, along with President Ronald Reagan, by John Hinckley who was armed with a handgun. Hinckley had hoped to impress actress Jodie Foster by his actions. He was mentally ill and had been harassing Foster for years.

Sarah Brady, James Brady's wife and the daughter of a Federal Bureau of Investigation agent, had for years worked for the banning of "Saturday night specials." These are cheap handguns, poorly made and so inexpensive that almost anyone can buy one. In some cities, Saturday night specials are the most common guns used in shootings, including accidental and deliberate ambushes, and drive-by attacks. Sarah Brady felt that banning the guns would prevent many shootings.

Sarah Brady changed the focus of her efforts to get gun control legislation enacted after her husband was accidentally shot (Hinckley was aiming only at President Reagan, but like many shooters, he missed and hit someone else in addition to his target). She now wanted a national system for checking the background of gun buyers. A dealer would take an order, check the buyer's identification, and then, over a period of a week, run the identification through a designated law enforcement agency. Anyone with a history of mental illness or who had been convicted of a felony would not be allowed to buy a gun.

Many people who were against gun control supported the Brady Bill. Although they believed that most bad guys could get around the effort at control by stealing, they did not object to a waiting period for gun buyers. And in a surprising number of instances, felons did try to legitimately buy guns and were refused. In 1994, the first full year after the Brady Bill was enacted into law, the Treasury Department did a random sampling of 441,545 handgun purchase applications. A total of 15,506 were denied because of the background check. And among the denials were applications from 4,365 felons.

Another benefit of the Brady Bill waiting period is that it gives some buyers a chance to rethink their purchase. There is anecdotal evidence, though no scientific statistics, showing that some people who register to

James Brady wears a "7 days can save a life" button, in support of the Brady Bill provision requiring a seven-day waiting period for a gun license. The actual bill provided for five working days.

buy a gun never return after the waiting period. Some of these people may have been angry with a family member, friend, coworker, or fellow student. They may have decided to buy a gun to either scare or shoot the person. If they could have gotten the gun in the heat of anger, someone may have been hurt. The waiting period allowed the angry person to calm down and think about what he or she had planned to do and the consequences. Then, when the anger was not so intense, the purchase seemed foolish. Similarly, a person in despair, if required to wait before getting a gun, may rethink a suicidal intention.

Most opponents of the Brady Bill were concerned about gun registration. This was not a requirement of the Brady Act, although the background check does make it possible to keep track of handgun purchases. In addition, many cities already have mandatory handgun registration laws, though most handgun owners never register their weapons. Some don't know about the registration requirement in their communities. Some feel the laws do not apply to handguns kept in the home (they do apply). And some claim that gun registration is the first step toward allowing a tyrant to take control of the country. If guns are registered, they say, a tyrant can order the police or the army to go to every home and confiscate them. This fear is one reason they want a weapon in the first place.

Two other gun control acts were passed in 1994. The 1994 Violent Crime Control and Law Enforcement Act banned the sale of nineteen different types of assault weapons. These are automatic or selective fire weapons intended for police and military use. Magazine clips holding more than ten rounds of ammunition were also banned. However, 670 makes and models of long guns used for hunting and sport shooting were exempted from the ban. Existing weapons in private homes were also exempted. The Youth Handgun Safety Act of 1994 was also passed. It prohibited possession of handguns by anyone under 18 years of age. In addition, someone giving or selling a handgun to a minor can go to jail for up to 10 years.

On November 30, 1998 the National Instant Criminal Background Check System (NICS) was put into operation by the FBI, as planned, replacing the Brady Bill plan. Gun dealers call a state number to check on a buyer's background. Some states have only criminal records in their computer database; others also have mental health records. Critics note that the new system fails to provide a cooling-off period for those buying a gun in anger.

High Tech Weapons

The availability of high tech weapons raises additional gun control issues. The Founders knew only one type of firearm, the slow-shooting, relatively inaccurate musket. Forcing members of a militia to own muskets was not a hardship because the same gun would be used for hunting, to provide wild game for the family dinner.

A gun shop employee shows two of the assault weapons banned by the U.S. Congress.

Today powerful weapons of war are available through many gun dealers. These include "street sweeper" shotguns, which can fire several shotgun shells in a few seconds, and automatic rifles, which can fire many rounds a minute. A burst from either type will practically disintegrate deer, and other game, making these weapons unusable for hunting. Their only purpose is to kill people; their design is for warfare.

Despite this, gun control opponents feel that such weapons should be available for anyone who desires them. They want no restrictions. Usually they argue that the buyers are either collectors or sport shooters or that, in today's society, these weapons will enable citizens to protect themselves against tyranny.

Advocates of unrestricted gun ownership often maintain that all modern handguns, rifles, shotguns, and even automatic weapons should be available to law-abiding citizens because of the Second Amendment. They see the musket as state-of-the-art weaponry of the late eighteenth century, the equivalent of automatic weapons and other high-powered firearms today. They feel that children should be trained in the use of these weapons so they will know how to handle them safely. Yet as James Brady has pointed out, for every instance where a gun kept in the home has been used to kill in genuine self-defense, forty-three people have died in accidents or as suicides involving such weapons. This statistic was confirmed in a 1986 study reported in the *New England Journal of Medicine*. Experts feel a study today would show even greater numbers of deaths in this manner.

Gun control advocates argue that all automatic weapons should be outlawed because they have no practical use other than to kill people. This is the same reason many want handguns outlawed, or their ownership severely restricted. The advocates argue that such controls would also prevent kids from gaining the means of attacking their classmates, families, neighbors, and themselves—attacks that are generating fear throughout the country.

How Bad Are Things Anyway?

Recent legislative acts have placed limitations on gun ownership. However these do not mean that you are safer than in the past. In 1995, a year after the passage of the Violent Crime Control and Law Enforcement Act, and the Youth Handgun Safety Act, a survey found that 5 percent of all students reported seeing a gun in their school, and 12 percent reported knowing a student who claimed to have brought a gun to school. That same year, 3,280 children and teenagers were murdered with guns (not all by other children). Another 1,450 committed suicide with guns, and 440 died in accidental shootings. This means that even with the laws tightened, 5,170 children and teenagers were killed by firearms in that year. This is an average of 14 children under the age of nineteen killed each and every day.[1]

In 1995, the volume of deaths by guns in the United States could be compared with figures from the Korean War. The Korean War, which your grandparents may have fought in, resulted in 33,651 American deaths during the more than two years of fighting. By contrast, in 1995, 35,957 Americans killed themselves and others with guns through homicides, suicides, and accidents in just the one year. An even more chilling comparison can be made with the Vietnam War, which lasted more than a decade. A total of 58,184 Americans died in Vietnam in all the years of fighting.[2] In the

United States, that many people are killed by guns in just two years.

As shocking as all this is, opponents of restrictions say that statistics are getting better. Handgun violence has actually decreased. For example, in 1992, more than 13,000 men, women, and children were killed by handguns in the United States. In 1996, handguns killed "only" 9,390.

The meaning of the decline is unclear. Some say it is the result of an aging population, because as people age, they become less likely to commit violence. Those who disagree with this explanation point out that four years is hardly long enough for a major change in the population to occur.

Some say that the decline in shootings reflects a decline in the use of illegal drugs in the United States. Handgun violence among blacks has declined, especially in inner cities where a corresponding decrease in drug use has been noted. At the same time, handgun violence among whites has slightly increased.

Still others feel that the statistics for the United States do not reflect the problem accurately. The 9,390 handgun deaths in 1996 must be compared with 106 fatal shootings in Canada (down from 128 in 1992), 30 in Great Britain (down from 33), 15 in Japan (down from 60). The United States had and has the highest rate of firearms-related deaths of children among the world's twenty-six richest nations. The Centers for Disease Control estimates that in the year 2003, gunshots will be the leading cause of death by injury— greater than car accidents, fires, and the like.

No matter what statistics show, many handgun owners share the beliefs of gun rights groups, such as the National Rifle Association. They state that criminals will always have weapons. Therefore it is only by having armed citizens that criminals will be afraid to commit crimes. Preventing citizens from owning one or more types of guns would embolden criminals into committing ever more violent acts. Some people feel they need to keep a handgun in their home to prevent criminals from trying to steal from them or hurting their families.

Some city governments agree with these ideas. Angered by the Brady Bill, officials in Kennesaw, Georgia, a suburb of Atlanta, passed an ordinance requiring all households to keep a gun and ammunition on hand at all times. This could be a handgun, rifle, or shotgun.

Other city governments feel that private gun ownership has drastically increased deaths and injuries, not because of criminal activity but because of accidental or deliberate violence within the home. Such communities, including the village of Morton Grove, Illinois, have banned all handgun ownership. Because only handgun ownership is outlawed, the ban does not

violate the wording or the spirit of the Second Amendment and has been upheld in Federal Court.

The state of Arizona allows any adult to carry a handgun so long as it is visible to everyone passing by. It is not unusual to see motorcycle riders traveling from Phoenix to the Grand Canyon with a clearly visible revolver or automatic handgun in a shoulder holster.

Reducing Gun Accidents

Some gun problems, such as accidental shootings caused by a person firing a gun when frightened, might be reduced if the owners had training in the care of their weapons and regular practice on a shooting range. Learning how to take care of weapons would help gun owners understand the potential dangers posed by having them in the home. Owners without weapons-training have injured themselves and others when they handled weapons they thought were safe. For example, some people remove an ammunition clip from an automatic and then think it is safe, not realizing a bullet may remain in the chamber. Revolver owners sometimes think the handgun is safe if there is no bullet under the firing pin. But the cylinder turns before the hammer falls, meaning the danger comes from the next round, not the one under the firing pin.

Practice shooting teaches self-control. Skilled shooters are alert to their targets and also to what they might hit if they miss. They are more likely to delay drawing or using a gun if there is a risk of hitting innocent bystanders. They also are more likely to wait until they are fully alert before pointing the weapon. They are aware, for example, that a home owner reaching for a bedside gun when hearing a noise in the house has a good chance of shooting a family member mistaken for an intruder. They may delay taking a potentially dead-

Gun safety instruction includes learning how to check to see if the gun is loaded, learning about the parts of the gun and how they work, and learning how to handle a gun.

ly action long enough to be certain they know the probable result of firing the weapon.

A few years ago one of the top handgun shooters in the nation, a member of the Phoenix, Arizona, police department, underwent a test simulating a home owner's possible experience. The officer lay on a bed, his revolver on a nightstand, and then let himself relax, drifting off toward sleep. The room was dark, but there was a light behind the closed bedroom door, and a human silhouette target was rigged to be visible when the door was opened.

Suddenly the door was opened, and the light from the hall filled the bedroom. The officer came alert, grabbed his revolver, and fired six rounds of ammunition at the target designed to look like an armed intruder. How many times did this top handgun expert hit the target in the test simulating a home owner's expected handgun use? Not one time.[3]

Was the police officer's reputation a fraud? Not at all. In fact, he was an expert on the best traditional firing range: the stress course. This is a range used by many police departments to simulate street conditions. There are pop-up targets of women carrying children, of teens and adults, of men with guns, and various combinations. The officer has to quickly identify the target as well as note any people around the bad guy. Sometimes there is a clear shot. Sometimes the officer has to wait to avoid hitting an innocent passerby, no matter what the bad guy is doing. This type of training is why so few innocent people are struck by bullets when police engage in a shoot-out.

Many gun owners who are skilled with their weapons and aware of the dangers demonstrated by the Phoenix police officer's test do not keep their handguns by their bed. Instead they find a place farther away, such as on a closet shelf, where it will take a little extra time to reach it. A few keep the gun unloaded in one part of the room and the bullets somewhere else, such as in a dresser drawer. They know that the time needed to awaken, leave their bed, and find and load the gun, will help them become fully alert before they consider using it. Their judgment will be better. Their control will be better. And they will be less likely to make a mistake.

Another problem that arises with too accessible handguns has to do with the "flight or fight" response. Have you ever been scared? Have you noticed that your heart beats faster and your body feels ready to run or attack someone? All your responses are speeded up, and if nothing happens, you are likely to sweat and to feel as if you are racing a bit as you calm down. This is the natural biochemical response to the release of adrenaline, the chemical that helps the body deal with trouble.

I first encountered the effects of adrenaline several years ago when I attended a police academy. I had been an expert shot with a rifle and had taught riflery. On my best day, I had been able to put bullet after bullet through the same dead-center hole on a small paper target fifty feet away. That was why I thought I would show off on my first day on the handgun range—even though the shooters had to fire at a life-sized human target while walking. Every few feet the range officer blew his whistle, and we quickly drew our guns and shot. We started at fifty yards and moved as close as nine feet. The course was intended to show us what stress can do, and it did. I missed every time.

Law enforcement officers practice to overcome the adrenaline rush and maintain control. (Yes, eventually I hit the target every time.) Controlling the stress is an essential skill for the streets where each radio call might mean trouble. This is different from the stress that comes from being awakened when you are asleep in your own bed. Adrenaline kicks in the same way, theoretically sharpening your ability to respond. But the ability to control it is lost during the first few moments when facing an unfamiliar situation.

This is why experts often say that a shotgun is the best weapon for home protection. The homeowner should assume he or she will miss, just as the police officer did. With a shotgun, each shell fires several pellets in a wide pattern. If the homeowner doesn't hit the target directly, one or more of the pellets will probably strike it. However, opponents of guns in the home note that the remaining pellets will keep going and can kill family members and pets. Again, the knowledge developed in ongoing training should convince the homeowner to keep the shotgun and shells far enough from the bed so that the homeowner will have to come to full alertness before acting. The danger still exists, but the knowledge may reduce the chance of a tragedy.

Another danger for the gun owner can be the weapon itself. The inexpensive handguns called Saturday night specials (thirty dollars or less when new, for example, compared with a similar-looking gun that might cost ten times that amount or more) are readily available. Some are made in Southern California; others are imported. What they share is poor construction, making them likely to misfire or otherwise not work. At times they injure the shooter. High school students who think they need to carry protection are frequently Saturday night special buyers. But the guns often fail to work properly and are extremely inaccurate.

Why Is it So Easy to Get Guns?

One source of guns is the gun show, an event held in cities and small towns throughout the nation. Some shows are small: perhaps two or three dozen dealers take booths to display their stock. Others are held in massive convention centers. Everything from Saturday night specials to sophisticated laser-guided weapons that look as if they were developed for action-adventure movies set many years in the future. They are meant for killing people, often at long distances, and have nothing to do with hunting or most forms of competitive target shooting.

At small, rural gun fairs, displays offer guns against a background of patriotism, commercialism, and vigilantism; with machine guns, ammunition, and propaganda presented by a variety of groups, sometimes including racists and survivalists.

At the world's largest gun show, in Las Vegas, Nevada, displays feature guns for hunting and target shooting, and for security.

Some displays feature survival manuals and containers of food for storage in case of a disaster or outbreak of war. Some dealers offer books on politics, history, or religion—many of an extremist nature. You can buy machine guns and fully automatic weapons, although if they are illegal to own fully assembled, you may have to go from display to display to buy individual parts, which are legal to own. You can also find books or individuals to guide you through the steps of assembling the weapon.

While some people go to gun shows to buy machine guns and automatic weapons, many of the visitors are seeking to purchase handguns without following the Brady Bill or the new Instant Check System. This is because there are two legal exceptions. One is a sale by a "vest pocket" dealer. This is someone who owns weapons he or she sells personally. The individual may wander the aisles of the gun show carrying several weapons, or they may be left in a hotel room to be brought out when someone is interested. If a price is agreed upon, the gun is sold for cash. No background check is made, no waiting period is observed, and usually no laws are broken. The Brady Bill and, now, Instant Check apply only to legitimate dealers, not individuals selling what they already own. But sometimes local ordinances expect registration of any handgun owned in the community. In those rare instances where a vest pocket dealer is arrested, it is not because he or she sold a gun. Rather it is almost always because sales tax was not collected as required in the city where the show was held.

The second exception through which a person may buy a gun without being checked is the estate sale. Guns that have been previously owned and that are part of an estate can be sold to anyone without observing a waiting period or a check. With both the estate sale and the vest pocket dealer, there is seldom a record of the transaction. It is cash only, requiring neither a background check nor a report to any authority.

A variation of the vest pocket dealer is the neighbor who collects guns and regularly sells or buys handguns and other weapons. Careful sellers limit their sales to friends, acquaintances, and coworkers they believe will handle the weapons safely. However, unlike the vest pocket dealer at a gun show where sales are legal, the neighbor may be violating zoning ordinances with such private sales.

President Bill Clinton has begun efforts to plug these loopholes that allow people to obtain guns without background checks.

Dishonest neighborhood dealers may make their sales in bars and other gathering places where they know some of the purchasers may plan to use the guns for crime. At the extreme are those who seek out gang members or youths in trouble with the law. The guns may be sold to them or rented by the day. The rental arrangement enables a person to be armed when desired, yet run a lower risk of being caught with a gun that can be connected to a crime.

Teenagers who have guns usually get them from a parent or family member, or through someone acting as a vest pocket dealer. Drew Golden got his first gun when he was six years old. It was a shotgun, a Christmas present he delighted in using on targets in a backyard shooting range. When he and Mitchell Johnson attacked their fellow students at Westside Elementary School, the guns they brought with them— a .38-derringer, a .38-snub-nosed revolver, and a .357 magnum—belonged to Drew's father. The first two were kept in a steel gun vault, locked and presumably safe. The third was left available in the open, for protection. The boys stole the rest of the weapons, four more handguns and three rifles, including a high-powered deer rifle, from Drew's grandfather's house where they were left in the open. The boys used a crowbar to break open the gun vault and to break into the grandfather's locked home.

Note: When Drew and Mitchell were convicted for their crimes, their sentences were based on their ages. They will be locked away until they are twenty-one years old, at which time they must be set free. All their rights will be restored. And even if the people who work in the juvenile prison feel they are still dangerous, they will have a legal right to own guns. Had they been old enough to be tried as adults, their sentences would have been much longer, and if they were ever released, they would never again have been legally able to buy or possess a gun. Even the court system is unsure how to handle the problem of kids and guns.

Kids Getting Guns

Kipland "Kip" Kinkel was fifteen and fascinated by guns. He lived in Springfield, Oregon, and in elementary school he liked to dress like a forest ranger. He was also unruly and his parents, both teachers, tried to find some way to get him interested in constructive activities. They wanted him to do better in his schoolwork. They wanted him to make friends. They wanted him to be more respectful.

Kip was so obsessed with guns that his father feared he would get himself one with or without family permission. His father decided that perhaps if he bought Kip a gun, his son would feel his parents cared about him. He also hoped the boy would learn to use it correctly.

Kip's parents were not hunters. Although Springfield is rural and gun ownership is fairly common, the older Kinkels were interested in tennis. They knew little about weapons and hoped only to please their son. So they gave him a .22-caliber semiautomatic rifle. Kip seemed so pleased that his father thought maybe they could help him by supporting his gun interest. He then bought the teen a Glock pistol, a weapon used by some law enforcement officers.

Kip was proud of his guns, so proud that he took the Glock to school to show off and was promptly expelled. His father, realizing he had made a mistake but wanting to help his son, arranged to send him to a National Guard program for troubled youths. The strict camp was meant to provide discipline and teach skills ranging from survival to proper weapons handling. It

A middle-school yearbook photograph of Kipland Kinkel, who is accused of opening fire in the school and killing one student and wounding many others.

seemed the ideal place for a boy who loved shooting but needed a firmer hand.

Kip was angry about being thrown out of school, an anger that grew to fury when his father told him he was going to be sent to the National Guard camp. Kip took one of his guns and shot his father through the head. Then, with chilling unconcern, he used the three-way calling feature on his telephone to talk with two friends about the episode of "South Park" on television that night. Kip loved the cartoon series and discussed the new episode with excitement. He never said that he had shot his father. He never said anything was wrong.

At 6 P.M., still on the telephone, Kip complained that his mother had not yet come home. He was hungry and wanted her to fix dinner. When she did arrive, he hung up. Then, by his own account, he told her he loved her, and shot her. That night he watched "South Park," and the next day he took his guns to school.

School Expulsions

The expulsion of Kip Kinkel demonstrated another difficult question for school administrators, teachers, and students. A number of schools have a zero-tolerance policy for anything declared to be a weapon—guns, knives, screwdrivers, and other items. A student who comes to school armed will be suspended or expelled, sometimes for a week, sometimes for several days, and sometimes for an entire year. This causes everyone who felt threatened by the student's possession of that weapon to feel safer. What was seldom considered in the past was what would happen when the student returns to school after the expulsion.

In the past, judges might have forced a student into a juvenile detention facility where little help was available. Or the judge might have ordered the youth to join the military if he or she was of appropriate age. However, the military put a stop to that practice when too many kids who had been in trouble in school were also found to be misfits in the military.

Today a growing number of school systems are experimenting with alternative ways to handle expelled students. Some require that the student enter counseling before returning. This may be aimed at helping the student with anger management or other issues which had earlier led the student to use violence as the only way to resolve his or her problems.

Some larger school systems have opened alternative schools for kids in trouble, either for carrying weapons or for causing other problems. The classes are frequently nontraditional and may enlist help from area businesses. For example, the school may be in a storefront in a downtown business district, as was tried in Tucson, Arizona, a number of years ago. The teachers at these schools try different approaches, working with all of the problems a student might have, not just learning problems. Or the nontraditional program may involve students in businesses that interest them. The students attend traditional classes for a half-day and work in the business the other half. For some this serves as a vocational education apprenticeship program, and successful students gain jobs after graduation. For others this becomes a way to explore careers for which they will go on to college or technical school. Always the teachers and counselors work with the issues in the students' personal lives that got them into trouble in the first place.

Back at a student's original school, classmates of the student who had the weapon often receive counseling. Many experienced shock and fear, and they may worry about how to react when the expelled student returns.

Bullet Control

New technology has made bullet control as controversial an issue as the ownership of guns. Ammunition manufacturers constantly work to develop new types of bullets to serve the needs of the military and law enforcement personnel. Some are meant to explode or split apart on impact, assuring that no matter where a person is struck, he or she will be too badly wounded to keep fighting. This type of ammunition includes the hollow point bullet, which is popular with police. It fragments on impact, sending bits of metal in all directions within the body of the person struck. A police officer who must shoot to protect his or her own life or the lives of others uses a hollow point to be certain the bad guy will be too hurt to keep fighting. Bullets that do not fragment can wound without stopping the attacker from shooting again. In wartime, with close-in fighting, exploding bullets do not continue traveling and so don't endanger friendly troops.

Other bullets are meant to penetrate anything that gets in the way. In the popular "Dirty Harry" movies starring Clint Eastwood, his detective character always carries a .44-magnum handgun, "the most powerful handgun in the world." He shoots people in stores. He shoots them on crowded streets. He shoots them wherever he finds them, and they always either die or end up spending weeks in the hospital.

The magnum bullets this fictional character uses—special high-powered bullets—are capable of shooting through a car's engine block or even bringing down big game in the wild. In truth, if police officers ever used .44-magnum bullets in a crowded city, they would probably kill half a dozen people or more. The bullet would pass through the target, through the walls of the apartment house, or other building, and through anyone in the way.

Any size bullet can be made with extra high power for its size. There are .22-caliber magnum bullets, for example. However, the most popular is the .357-magnum, a bullet the same size as the common .38-caliber bullet used in revolvers favored by police officers and home gun enthusiasts. The .357-magnum is approximately the size of the 9 mm bullet used in the automatics now issued to many police officers. These guns are favored because they hold approximately fifteen rounds of ammunition compared with the five or six rounds of the standard .38-caliber revolver.

A handgun made to shoot a magnum load is designed to handle greater heat and force than one that will shoot only .38-caliber bullets. Police favor them when they have patrol duty that may take them into isolated areas without backup. For exam-

The actor Clint Eastwood, in the role of Dirty Harry, takes aim with his trademark .44-magnum handgun.

ple, one sheriff's deputy told me that he uses a .357-magnum revolver as his sidearm, carrying three types of bullets to match his needs. When patrolling in the city, he uses standard .38-caliber bullets. When patrolling rural stretches of highway he switches to .357-magnum loads so he can stop a car by shooting through the engine block if necessary. And when working in an area amusement park, he loads with snake shot to limit the danger to the crowd should he miss if he ever has to shoot.

Bullet manufacturers recently added the nonstick coating Teflon to some bullets. Teflon-coated .38-caliber bullets have a greater penetrating power than standard bullets with the same power. And .357-magnums penetrate further as well. The problem is that a Teflon-coated bullet can penetrate a police officer's bullet-resistant vest. Police call the Teflon-coated ammunition "cop killer bullets," and many want it to be illegal to sell the ammunition to anyone outside of the military and law enforcement. Yet, as there are people who want freedom to own any type of weapon, so there are those who want to be able to buy every type of bullet that will fit their guns. As a result, the more extreme bullets, totally inappropriate for hunting or self-defense, create a moral and business dilemma for the gun dealers. If they refuse to sell them, the potential buyers will find other dealers who will supply the legal but unusually dangerous ammunition. Then those buyers are likely to make their gun purchases with the new dealers as well.

If the dealer chooses to sell the highly specialized bullets, the buyers can do tremendous harm with them. Anyone shooting such a bullet, no matter what his or her intentions, can accidentally kill or wound several individuals after hitting the target. Despite the fact that they are unsuitable for hunting and self-defense, there are people who buy them and keep them in their homes.

Some buyers of these extreme forms of ammunition want to shoot it at ranges that have appropriate back-stops, just to see what it is like. Some collect bullets in the same manner as they collect guns. And some fear that the American government is changing radically. They fear the possibility of a dictatorship and claim that to preserve democracy, the average citizen needs adequate weapons to fight evil and to intimidate those who would dare come against them. The specialized bullets are part of what they feel should be a citizen's arsenal.

Are Guns the Only Problem?

Many critics of gun control point out that teenagers carry an assortment of weapons. Someone ready to do violence may use a knife, a club, or even a screwdriver. In fact, in areas where security measures have almost eliminated the chance that a student can bring a gun into school, students say the screwdriver is the weapon they see most frequently. Teens know it can be deadly, but teachers unfamiliar with violence may dismiss the tool as harmless. Only the students know the danger, and in many parts of the country, they do not talk about it to teachers or other adults. They maintain a "code of silence," a problem discussed in the next chapter.

Of all the variety of makeshift weapons carried by students who are scared or who want to impress their classmates, the gun is the most deadly. It can be used at a distance. If the bullet misses its intended victim, it can travel for well over a mile, striking anyone in its path. And a gun is most likely to leave the victim badly injured, paralyzed, or dead. That is why guns are so troubling to those who feel the Second Amendment is being interpreted incorrectly and at the expense of children and young adults.

A rally by Citizens Against Gun Violence featured a "Chain of Remembrance," with linked panels commemorating victims of gun violence.

Chapter 5
The Code of Silence

The young adult years are often a time of experimentation and rebellion. This can be both good and bad. It is a time of weighing family values, experiencing new emotions, taking on adult responsibilities, and enjoying new freedoms. Yet there is still the protection of home and school, familiar safe places where adults assume ultimate responsibility.

Failing to explore the unfamiliar can be limiting. Part-time jobs help you learn about responsibility, your importance to others, how to work with people of different ages and backgrounds, and how to manage money, among other benefits. To never question the way you have been living while in school would be to never leave home. This is the time to try new things and make mistakes while there is still a safety net.

Experimentation also has a dark side. During these years, you and the kids you know may have made good choices based on understanding that it is best not to try things you know are harmful. Or you may have considered experimenting with alcohol, drugs, cigarettes, and similarly destructive and sometimes illegal activities, or with sexual activities that carry risks and responsibilities. You have choices. Sometimes what you choose determines whether or not you get hurt. You are aware of the risks and the consequences in experimenting. And if you have strong feelings about a friend's experimentation, you may have talked with that person yourself.

This is natural and normal. You want to establish your own identity with your own generation. You are trying to learn about unfamiliar career possibilities, how to handle relationships, and other concerns. You are trying to act in a mature manner, speaking up when you see something wrong happening with someone you care about.

The process of establishing your own identity separate from the adults in your life is sometimes responded to in a negative way. Sometimes adults give the impression that they don't want to hear negative stories about the teens for whom they are partly responsible. This is especially true with some schoolteachers and administrators.

A few years ago I interviewed a number of kids from age eleven through seventeen who were alcoholics. They lived in Tucson, Arizona, which, at the time, had the largest Teen AA (Alcoholics Anonymous) chapter of any city in the United States. These kids had recognized their problem and were working to get over it.

The teenagers told me that there was a serious problem at a high school considered one of the finest public schools in the area. Almost all of the school's students graduated and went on to college, many with partial or full scholarships. They had award-winning programs in the arts, and their athletic programs were among the best in the state. But at least twenty or more of the students had drinking problems the principal refused to acknowledge.

I visited the high school and spoke to the students and the principal. The students talked about kids who brought alcohol to school; sneaking drinks between

A student anti-gun rally

classes, during lunch breaks, and after school. They made it clear it was no secret, and they also said they didn't think anyone cared.

The principal stated that the school had no problem with kids and alcohol, so I told him what I had heard. He then admitted that kids had been caught drinking in school. "But we expel them immediately. They are off campus the moment we catch them," the principal said.

"Don't you have a counseling program? Don't you help them deal with this?"

"Our concern is education," was the response. "They know the rules. They drank. They're out of here. We can't have them corrupting the good students."

The principal was concerned about being seen by the parents, the school superintendent, and the school board, as a successful administrator. He felt that to acknowledge problems with students was to admit he wasn't as good as they expected. Rather than risk his job by discussing the problems, he expelled any student who might be difficult.

Note: Technically a principal does not expel a student. There is a procedure involving the school board in order to protect the student's rights. However, some principals and school boards do not work that way in practice. Whatever the principal recommends is rubber-stamped by the board members.

The students stopped trusting the principal. Unfortunately, the teachers who knew what was happening with the troubled students did not challenge the policy. Students who went to them for help with their own problems or those of friends found the teachers ignored their pleas. Eventually the students felt that they had to work together, no matter how limited their knowledge and resources, because they couldn't get help from the people they should have been able to trust. And when they knew a teen was in trouble, they would try to protect him or her from discovery. The system was failing.

Students try to protect other students everywhere. You probably have friends or acquaintances who have experimented with what adults call "self-destructive behavior." Maybe they have shoplifted, or gotten drunk, or tried drugs. Maybe they have discussed sexual experimentation that you feel is wrong. Maybe they have talked about being depressed, feeling extremely sad, perhaps feeling that everyone hates them and they would be better off not living. And maybe some have talked about killing others or getting back at those who have hurt them.

Protecting friends often leads to a code of silence, the unwritten rule that keeps students from telling adults what is really happening. This is proving increasingly deadly throughout the United States. And it is not just a student problem. As you will see in Chapter 8, teachers are often unprepared to take students seriously and listen to them. Every school needs to develop a mechanism, or a system, to ensure that students are listened to, and heard. In addition, students must be guaranteed anonymity. No student wants to be called a "squealer," a "tattletale," a "rat." Yet for your own sake, the sake of your friends and your classmates, a way to break the code of silence has to be developed.

No matter what difficulties you may be facing with parents and teachers, maintaining the code of silence can cost you your health, your future plans, or your life. The code of silence is ultimately as deadly as any handgun when you know a kid is planning an act of violence.

Chapter 6

Why Are Kids Killing Other Kids?

No one knows exactly why one child goes on a shooting spree while another child, with a similar background, does not. Both may be troubled at home and unpopular at school; but one turns to violent action and the other does not. Some experts suggest that television and motion pictures are factors. Many shows feature violence, often to increase their teen audience. Summer action-adventure movies, with their high-speed car chases, endless gunplay, frequent explosions, and martial arts combat between the hero and the bad guys, are directed at males from fourteen to twenty-four. The hero is often the loner with a gun—the person who acts in ways others consider reckless or improper—who saves the girl, the world leader, the high-rise building, the ship, the airplane, or whatever else is in danger. The hero will shoot, bomb, or do whatever is necessary to stop the bad guys, always ignoring traditional law enforcement officers. Even cartoon and cartoon-like programs aimed at younger children carry a violent message. In preschools across America boys and girls delightedly "karate kick" in imitation of the Mighty Morphin Power Rangers or the Teenage Mutant Ninja Turtles.

The "Teenage Mutant Ninja Turtles"

Television and Movie Violence

Writers for television know that they must constantly think about the visual impact of what they create. The two most visceral experiences humans share are sex and violence. This is why sex and violence—which both carry great visual impact—are used as primary components of many television programs. The Center for Population Options determined in one study that teenage television-watchers see almost 14,000 sexual encounters every year. A 1992 study published in the *Journal of the American Medical Association* stated that the average child watches television twenty-seven hours a week. He or she will watch 40,000 murders and 200,000 other acts of violence by the age of eighteen. The Center for Media and Public Affairs had monitors watch all network and cable channels available in Washington, D.C., for just one day, April 7, 1994. The body count was 2,605 acts of violence on that one day alone.

It is easy to say that these shows are fantasy, that children know the difference. But is that the truth? Dr. Martin Reiser, the first police psychologist for the Los Angeles Police Department, described a situation in which a four-year-old girl seemed to have witnessed a murder that took place in the next apartment. A man went to see the woman next door to the child. They argued in her bedroom, and he drew a gun and shot her, all in plain view of the child, who told officers she was looking out the window.

Certainly the crime scene matched what the child said. The victim's body was in her bedroom. She had been killed by gunshots. And other witnesses had seen a man enter the building to visit the victim. It seemed that the officers had an eyewitness to the killing, which could possibly speed the arrest and conviction of the murderer.

The detectives had the child take them into the bedroom where she had been playing when the shooting took place. As she described, there was a window and while it did not look directly into the apartment next door, it seemed possible that the child, leaning out, could have a clear view. Then the little girl took the detectives to the "window" through which she had been looking. It was a wall-mounted television set which the little girl thought was a window. By coincidence, she had been watching a television movie in which a woman was murdered in her bedroom. A check with the

Cartoon and live action programs bombard young viewers with scenes of violence.

television station broadcasting the movie found that the scene of the murder in the film occurred at approximately the same time as the shooting.

"We discovered that a four-year-old child cannot tell the difference between a television and a window," Dr. Reiser explained. Is it any wonder that some children come to think that television shows reflect real life?

A recent study by sociologists at Case-Western Reserve University found that children who watch more than four hours of television a day tend to be far more aggressive and violent than children who see less television. Other researchers have found that both heavy television viewing and the prolonged playing of violent video games have the same effect.

What is not known is whether the children come to mimic the violence they see because they think this is appropriate behavior, or whether disturbed children reinforce their behavior patterns through viewing so much violence.

Can the same observation of more aggressive behavior be seen with adult viewers? During the Vietnam War, the nightly news was often filled with scenes of what were called firefights, shooting the enemy in the jungle. The camera crews captured the violence, the fear, the sudden death on both sides.

Each night the news segued into entertainment. Gunfire in Vietnam switched to gunfire in action pictures. Surveys at the time indicated that a surprisingly large number of people could not separate in their minds film coming from the war zone and the entertainment that followed.

There was also a concern that the news broadcasts were desensitizing viewers to violence. News shows were often broadcast at 6 P.M., and it was not unusual for a family's dinner hour to be centered on the television. A few years earlier TV dinners were invented for families with too little time to cook. Then TV trays were introduced, and many families got into the habit of watching the news while eating.

Over the last two to three decades, a number of parents have tried to show that crimes were directly related to television.[1] In 1976, when a nine-year-old girl was assaulted by students in her California elementary school, her mother claimed the attack was directly related to one shown in the NBC movie *Born Innocent*. The lawsuit, which the networks feared and which took six years to go to court, ended abruptly. The attorney for the mother could not prove that the boys involved in the assault had been influenced by the movie.

A similar situation occurred in the case of Randy Zamora, a fifteen-year-old Florida boy. He broke into a woman's house and killed her and then pleaded insanity based on "prolonged, intense, involuntary, subliminal television intoxication."[2] In other words, the television made him do it.

Testimony was heard that Zamora watched endless crime shows. He shaved his head so that he would look like Kojak, a popular television detective played by the bald actor Telly Savalas. A psychiatrist testified that the boy had seen so many acts of violence where there were no bad consequences that he did not understand the reality of what he was doing when he shot the woman.

What did the jury say? They felt that Zamora was nothing more than a teenager who planned a robbery and then committed murder in the course of carrying it out. In their minds, television had nothing to do with it.

By the 1990s, despite some inconclusive cases, Dr. William Dietz of the American Academy of Pediatrics told a congressional committee that television violence had a clear and "reproducible" effect on children. It especially influenced the way they chose to solve problems among themselves.[3] They would use fistfights, kicking, and other forms of physical aggression instead of trying to work out their differences. They often felt threatened by others, thinking that they had to fight to avoid being hurt even though there was nothing in the actions of the other children to give that impression.

Violent television, movies, and video games are not the only factors that contribute to violence in kids according to other researchers. Gil Noam, professor of education and medicine at Harvard University, has been quoted as saying, "Many boys have impulse-control problems. They don't think, 'What are going to be the consequences for the rest of my life?'"

Many parents argue that kids have always acted out, fantasized, and threatened violence. The ancient philosopher Plato bemoaned the fact that kids were dis-

At a video-game arcade, players drop bombs in a video-simulated desert.

respectful to their parents, acting out, and otherwise behaving as you and your friends sometimes do. The difference is the relative accessibility of guns and a desensitization to the potential pain of others. Television and movie violence does not show the horror, pain, and long-term suffering of being shot, stabbed, or beaten.

The Advertising Industry

Some observers think we must examine the advertising industry when discussing whether or not television influences kids to commit crimes with guns. Companies pay hundreds of millions of dollars to place their fifteen-second, thirty-second, and one-minute advertisements in the midst of popular television shows. To pay for these advertisements, and for the costs of development and manufacturing, and for the salaries of the people involved with the creation of a new cereal, athletic shoes, cars, and everything else they advertise, they have to sell more.

How much more? If Captain Cavity Cereal is created and packaged in a colorful box decorated with the Mr. Toothrot Action Figure, a commercial is made to introduce it to the public—the consumer. A studio is rented, a director is hired, along with a sound crew, film crew, lighting technicians, set designers, casting agent, and actors. The production costs for the Captain Cavity Cereal commercial equal the costs of a half-hour situation comedy. When you add the cost of placing the advertisement in children's cartoon shows, the manufacturer will have spent as much money as an independent film producer spends for a feature film shown at the Sundance Film Festival. Now suppose the cereal sells for $2.50 per box when it is introduced in stores. When you subtract the cost of the distributors' and the retailers' percentages of the selling price, it may take a million boxes of the new cereal just to meet the cost of advertising. And far more have to be sold to produce a profit.

Are the odds bad? Is this like playing the lottery? No. After more than fifty years of television advertising, companies know that the best way to sell a product, a person (such as a politician), or an idea is through television. You, the consumer, will believe the advertising. You, the consumer, will do what the advertiser asks. Television is so "real" and so trusted that it is the perfect vehicle for influencing how you think and what you do.

If television advertising is so powerful, it is impossible to believe that television programs do not influence behavior. Yet that is what producers and programming executives want you to think. A television movie can show teenagers killing their friends, classmates, or family, and the apologists in the industry will say, "All teens understand this is pretend. They know the difference. They know this behavior is wrong. They would never get upset and do it themselves. They aren't influenced by what they see at all." Then those same industry executives will tell businesses that if they advertise during those shows, the viewers—you and your friends—will believe whatever they see in the advertisements.

What's shown on the screen has even greater impact on the loner who uses television for a friend. He or she relates to the actors as real people. The loner learns how to behave from watching how the characters behave. Then he or she acts accordingly, sometimes finding it was the right way, sometimes getting ridiculed or experiencing serious problems.

For example, you may have heard of date rape. You may even know someone who experienced this nightmare. What you may not be aware of is that when adults commit date rape, it is often because they are loners who are modeling their behavior on what they have seen in movies. Radio talk show host and author Tonya Flynt-Vega, the daughter of self-described pornographer Larry Flynt (*Hustler* magazine), discovered one connection between pornography and date rape when researching her book *Hustled: My Journey from Fear to Faith*.[4]

•

One common theme in some readily rentable pornographic videos is that a woman says "no" when she means "yes." The man is supposed to not take "no" for an answer. Instead, he will force himself on her, overpowering her, perhaps restraining her, perhaps hitting her. Instead of being terrified and badly hurt as she is in real life, the actress is shown as suddenly desiring the man. She becomes an aggressively willing partner.

The man who has learned his dating skills in this way is usually taking out a friend from school or work. He has dated little or not at all, and this relationship is special because it is with a friend. It is likely to include private time away from others where they might kiss and touch, sharing a closeness that started as a friendship. Then, if the man starts to go further, the woman may say "no," it is not the time for anything else. They need to know each other better. She had a wonderful evening, but it is time to go to their separate homes.

The loner raised on pornography has heard a variation of this line in the videos he has rented or seen on some late night cable television shows. He becomes more aggressive. She resists. He "knows" this means she wants him and he acts accordingly. He truly attacks her, raping her, then is shocked to find her weeping, angry, perhaps fighting him violently. When he is arrested, he is often confused as to why. He doesn't realize until then that, in her eyes, he was doing something wrong.

•

Yet television executives claim that when teens watch violent crime shows, they are not being influenced.

This is not to say that you will become violent from watching such action shows. However, if a teen, perhaps even a friend or classmate of yours, is troubled, angry, and looking for a way to get back at those he or she thinks have hurt him or her, obsessive watching of violent programs can lead to trouble.

Television does not create a Luke Woodham or the other children who have taken guns to school. But television can be one factor in convincing a child or teenager that using a gun is a valid way to settle differences or solve problems.

The Music Industry

Other forms of popular culture also have an influence on how you behave. The music industry is probably the best example, especially when it comes to violent rap and rock music. While "gangsta rap" glorifying antipolice and, often, antiwoman sentiment is usually targeted for blame here, for years a surprising number of rock songs have been both antiwoman and pro-gun. Battering, rape, and murder have been themes of some of the songs.

But does listening to such music really matter? The Parents Music Resource Center, founded by Tipper Gore, the wife of Vice President Al Gore, thinks it does. However, the first person to examine the premise through scientific testing of more than four thousand individuals was Dr. John Kappas of Van Nuys, California.[5]

Dr. Kappas, a long-time therapist and researcher, was hired by Capitol Records in 1962 to see if the "back masking" of a record could get people to respond to a hidden message. The back-masking technique became possible with the then new technology of multi-track recording.

"Suppose we had twelve tracks on which to record the music and the lyrics," explained Sandy Sharmat, a retired recording engineer. "To back mask we would record tracks one through ten and track twelve in the normal way. Then we would flip the reel so that track eleven became track two. We would record this new track two with whatever someone wanted to say on it, then flip the tape back as we had it at first. When you heard the whole tape played normally, the backwards message really couldn't be heard. At least I never thought so. But what did I know?"

Dr. Kappas explained that the idea behind back masking is that the brain somehow hears the backwards message, remembers it, and somehow turns it around to hear it correctly. Then it later influences the listener's behavior.

For example, suppose the back-masked message is "Buy more rock music records." It would be heard as "sdrocer cisum kcor erom yub." Your subconscious mind would hear it and mentally reverse the words. The focus on the back–masked message that was necessary to reverse the message would cause you to remember it and act on it when you were in a store.

"The record company thought they could get the listener to buy more records. The Beatles were just becoming big back then, and Paul McCartney thought this might help them sell more of their albums," explained Dr. Kappas. "Instead, most people never heard the back-masked message. We tested over four thousand people and only the most sensitive were aware of the odd sound. They just thought it was noise."

Back masking was a flop, though it continues to be tried by a wide range of recording artists. However, curious to see if records could influence behavior, Dr. Kappas continued the research on his own. What he discovered may be a factor in why some kids act out violent ideas in some music. "We learned that lyrics could have an unusually strong influence if they were recorded slightly softer than the music so you would have to listen closely to hear them. Then, if you added sensory deprivation, they would have even stronger impact."

Dr. Kappas explained that sensory deprivation could be achieved by wearing earphones. Today Walkman-style tape players and earphones are as common among kids and young adults as athletic shoes. Because they focus your attention on the music and not on the sounds of the people, cars, and general noise all around, they provide the sensory deprivation Dr. Kappas discussed.

"The lyrics heard in this way won't convince you to do something you wouldn't normally do," said Dr. Kappas. He mentioned the example of the parents who sued a musician and record company after their teenage son killed himself. He had been listening repeatedly to the song "Suicide Solution" before taking his own life. "Instead, they will cause you to take seriously an idea you would normally not consider. In the case of suicide, someone who does not believe in suicide will not take his or her life because of a song. But with the lyrics softer than the music and the song heard through earphones, the listener might jokingly say, 'Well, I could always kill myself.' The listener won't do it. But without the song heard that way, the listener probably would not have had the thought."

Do the record company executives think about this? Do they care? One disturbing situation was revealed when Time Warner, Inc. was producing records by a group called Nine Inch Nails. One of the songs was "Big Man with a Gun," with lyrics that included foul language and the singer talking of shooting someone after forcing the person to engage in a sex act.

The song was so offensive that William Bennett, the former secretary of education, and C. Delores Tucker, the head of the National Political Caucus of Black Women, met with a group of Time Warner executives, including chairman Gerald M. Levin. The two were outraged by the violent content of music meant for young people and insisted that copies of the lyrics, which they had brought with them, be read aloud by each of the executives. None of them were willing to do it. They were making money on songs with messages so violently obscene that none of them would speak the words aloud. How extreme might be the reaction of a youth in crisis whose focus is on such music?

One of the early signs that a troubled youth needs help is when listening to a song or type of song becomes obsessive. The same song is played over and over again. The listener thinks of little else, focusing on the idea of the lyrics. If the lyrics are about suicide, the teen may use them to justify taking his or her own life. If they are about doing violence to others, again the listener hears justification.

But the key word is obsessive. This is not about loving a particular group or having a favorite song you like to sing a lot. This is being so focused on one song or one idea in the lyrics that you listen to almost nothing else. It plays in your head, over and over. Your grades go down. Your past friendships become unimportant. You may start hanging out only with kids who talk the same way, who think the same way. Often these are kids you once avoided.

Kyle Foster, one of the Pearl, Mississippi, teenagers allegedly targeted by Luke Woodham, talks about the "kids in black." All the boys and girls with whom Luke Woodham was involved before the shooting deliberately set themselves apart from the more popular athletes and active members of various arts programs. They dressed in black, again an action that called attention to themselves and made them appear different. They often talked about nontraditional religions, such as Satanism and pagan activities, and extremist political philosophies. "They weren't part of the popular groups," said Kyle, a football player and school leader. "We never had much to do with them."

This is not to say that all the "kids in black" were or are dangerous. Although two other boys were allegedly going to be involved with violence at Pearl High, only Luke showed up with a gun. But his involvement with a group of social outcasts, at least by the standards of the more popular students, is typical of some of the kids who have chosen either gun violence against others or suicide.

Fantasy and Role-Playing Games

Fantasy and role playing games can have an impact similar to that of obsessive music lyric interest. These games became extremely popular beginning with Dungeons & Dragons several years ago. In fact, the Phoenix, Arizona, public schools encouraged the use of fantasy role-playing games as an aid to creative learning. The problem for some kids was that they became obsessed with the game. They played every chance they could. When their friends tired of it or wanted to play basketball, go to a movie, hang out at the mall, do anything else for a few hours, those friends were dropped. The obsessed player found other kids, equally obsessed, to share the interest.[6]

"For some kids, the fantasy game became so real they would 'take it off the board,'" explained retired police captain Dale Griffis, Ph.D., who has trained more than 38,000 law enforcement officers throughout the United States.[7] "They may take their own lives or someone else's. Their obsession with the game has made them think it is real, the imaginary powers are within their reach if they just perform the right ritual."

In one instance, a nineteen-year-old boy took a hammer late one night and attacked his younger brother, and then turned and attacked his father. He allegedly was trying to kill everyone in his family as part of the role-playing game that, for him, had become real.

When the father subdued his son and the police investigated, they found that the attacker had become obsessed with the game two years earlier. His grades had dropped dramatically, and he had barely graduated, although he had previously been a top student. He lost a series of part-time jobs because he would talk only about the game. He kept what is sometimes called a "book of shadows" by people involved with the occult. It was a notebook in which he recorded "spells" he believed had brought him power. Somewhere in his thinking the game had become reality; reality a game, and his character had to take lives to win. That was when he attacked his younger brother and his father.

A similar situation occurred in the Denver, Colorado, region a few years ago, though with a different ending. The boy who became obsessed left a diary in which he reported selling his soul to the Devil and promising to take the lives of others in order to gain invisibility and the power to call forth fire from his fingers. His diary indicated that he felt himself becoming crazy. Then he decided that he was comfortable in his self-created world. Finally, certain he had to take a life but unable to kill anyone else, he killed himself.

Tragically, several other kids, equally obsessed with the game, also took their own lives. In every instance there had been warnings that their friends, parents, and teachers all saw, but none of them intervened.

The Internet

The Internet is also believed to be a factor when kids take up guns to hurt others. This is not because the Internet is inherently evil. It is not because there are dangers lurking there. However, it has been seen that the Internet can provide a highly disturbed, withdrawn loner with a supportive "family" who may encourage his or her violent fantasies.

You are reading this book because you are concerned about kids and guns. You or a family member might own a gun. You might like hunting or target shooting. Or you might live in a household with no guns, where the idea of owning a gun goes against your family's values. Whatever the situation, you are aware of a danger from kids and guns. You have heard of some school shootings. You may have seen or heard about kids taking weapons to school. And you consider what has happened in other areas to be frightening and wrong.

Perhaps you have discussed the shootings in school, or with your family and friends. Most likely you have been horrified. Certainly this violence is something you would never commit. The idea goes against everything you have learned at home, at school, and in any religious group. However, for an unhappy loner—troubled, obsessed, and potentially violent—the Internet creates a very different environment. An Internet chat room can become a place where loners gather to support one another's violent ideas.

Many critics of the use of the Internet by children and teenagers point to the ease with which anyone can gain access to obscene and other inappropriate material. They are distressed that young people may see photographs of perversions that most adults find offensive. They also fear that in chat rooms, an occasional sexual predator may tell lies to obtain pictures or arrange meetings with children and teens who think they are talking to someone their own age.

What Dr. Griffis and other researchers have found is that for some obsessed loners, Internet chat rooms can provide the "friends" they do not have in school. On the Internet there are always individuals who will support even the most outrageous behavior. They may do it as a joke, or they may do it because they are serious about wanting to act out violently and they seek the support they cannot find in their home communities.

For example, one bulletin board has information about counterculture activities: How to make explosives; how to make a device for obtaining free long distance telephone calls; how to break into computer files for the purpose of damaging them. This bulletin board also posts stories of crime. One writer described his exploits with two friends, and told how they break into homes late at night and attack the sleeping residents.

The "memoirs" of teens and young adults claiming to act out violently against neighbors, classmates, teachers, and others are not ones most people will read for pleasure. They are often obscenely graphic. They may also be true. In a few instances they have matched actual incidents police have investigated.

What may matter most is that the stories encourage other teens and young adults to live out their violent fantasies, going out into their own communities to do whatever gives them pleasure. After they have committed the crimes, they write up their experiences and place them on the bulletin board for other browsers to read.

What is the impact of such a bulletin board? "Many potentially violent loners would never go further than sick fantasy without some sort of support," explains Dr. Griffis. "They can't get it [support] at home, at school, or at work. Often they look and act different so people in their communities are already wary of them. But when they obsessively go on the Internet, they can fantasize that they are part of a real community of like-minded friends. They feel they are normal, that a large number of people think as they do. With the support of people they've never met, who may even be playing a sick joke, they are willing to act violently when, without that support, they would never cross that line."

Other Triggers

In some areas, especially where there are gangs, using a gun is like a rite of passage. "They told me I had to

Youth gang initiation rites sometimes include violence

shoot someone to be a member," said Jimmy, now twenty-one and working in a Los Angeles restaurant while attending college. He had moved to the area from Illinois after his father died in a car accident and he and his mother moved in with her sister living in California.

•

It was stupid, but I didn't think I had anything else. My mother and aunt both worked, you know? The apartment was in one of those places where everybody's like twenty-five with two or three little kids running around or they're all so old, they tell you to turn down your music when you're wearing headphones. I hung out on the streets, and when you hang out where I did, you either get in a gang or you get beaten up a lot.

Not that the gang kept you safe. You go over on one street and the Rolling Sixes will jump you. You go on another and you got to watch out for the Crips. You're running scared all the time, even when you're in the gang. But I figured with the gang I had family, a place to go.

They told me I had to prove myself. They said I had to shoot someone because then I'd have a secret only they would know. I'd have to trust them not to tell the cops just like they had to trust me when they did it. So they gave me this revolver with five bullets and I hid it inside my pants, under my shirt.

I swaggered out of there like I was some bad dude. But inside I was scared, really scared. Guns are cool on television. Everybody waving them around. People scared of you. Like you're the man.

I went home when my mother and my auntie were at work, and I stood by the mirror, practicing drawing the gun. I was going to keep it on me until I was in some neighborhood where I knew there was a rival gang. I figured I'd maybe go early in the morning where anyone I saw might be alone. No one around. And I'd draw my gun and just blow him away. It wasn't really like hurting anybody. I'd just stand a few feet away and shoot him. Nothing personal.

Dumb. I know. That's how I was thinking as I practiced jerking the gun out of my pants and pointing it at the mirror. I didn't know anything about guns. I figured you kept your finger on the trigger when drawing it. I figured that's what cops did. I didn't know how easy it is to pull the trigger when you're tense, scared.

It must have been the third or fourth time I drew that gun when it went off. I mean the bullet tore down my leg making a crease in my jeans. It was hot as hell as it tore off the skin and shot off the tip of one of my toes. The doctor told me I was lucky I didn't hit an artery. Said I might have bled to death. He said I could have screwed up my foot as well. Maybe never walked again.

Scared me, man. I'm still scared just thinking about it. But I was lucky. I was too dumb to think about the consequences until after I pulled the trigger. I might have killed someone. Gone to jail for the rest of my life. It was all so stupid.[8]

•

Jimmy left the neighborhood. His mother said she had had enough when she learned what happened. She and her sister moved to where nobody knew Jimmy, nobody made him feel he had to join a gang to be safe. He went to court for discharging a firearm in the city, a misdemeanor. "I got lucky. Real lucky."

Gun Sources

The sources for handguns are many. They are available in inner cities, wealthy suburban areas, and rural farm communities. Many are cheap. Few are properly maintained. And too many are available to children with no knowledge of the proper handling.

Some communities are passing laws holding parents responsible for the proper storage and safety of handguns they own. They are expected to keep the weapons in a location where their children cannot gain access to them. The parents are considered accessories if their children take the guns and use them in any illegal manner.

Lawmakers know that even the best safety precautions a parent takes can often be overcome by a determined kid. There have been instances when a child stole a gun-safe key long enough to have a copy made. Kids have used car tire changing tools to pry open locked gun cabinets. However, what the lawmakers are doing, in addition to forcing parents to take precautions, is forcing them to reconsider gun ownership. Do they want to have a weapon at home if they know they could go to jail for the actions of one of their children?

The hope is that fewer people will want to buy guns when they know the problem. This is also why many gun clubs now maintain lockers to hold the weapons for members who enjoy competitive target shooting. The owners can leave the guns at the club instead of keeping them at home where they might be misused.

All of this raises two important issues: How should handguns and other weapons be handled if your parents own them or they are found in the homes of your friends? And what can you do to be safe from kids with guns at your school?

Tragedy can occur even when it is not deliberate and a weapon seems safe. In Oakland, California, fifteen-year-old Kenzo Dix was killed by a Beretta handgun he and a fourteen-year-old friend were examining. Both boys understood the danger of handguns. Both boys thought they were acting responsibly when they carefully removed the ammunition clip from the gun. But when the fourteen-year-old pulled the trigger, the gun fired. There had been a bullet in the chamber, unnoticed by the boys who thought removing the clip meant no bullets were left in the gun. There was no way for them to tell the handgun was still loaded, so Kenzo died and his friend's life was changed forever.

Other teens have also been shot in tragic accidents. In West Monroe, Louisiana, a fourteen-year-old girl planned to trick her parents. She told them that she was staying overnight in a friend's house. Then she hid in a closet and came out at midnight to play her joke. Terrified, her father grabbed the gun he kept to protect his family and fired, killing his daughter.

Local groups often sponsor events aimed at ending gun violence. A "Gun Turn In Day" sponsored by the Enough is Enough Organization netted 161 weapons and 50 pounds of ammunition.

Chapter *7*

Gun Safety

The Basics of Gun Safety

Guns have long been a part of the American culture. Whether they are purchased for protection or for hunting or collected as a hobby, they are all around us. They might be in your home or the home of a friend or classmate. As a result, it is critical that you understand the basics of handling a gun safely and protecting people from weapons kept in the home.

1. "Guns are always loaded."

You must always assume that a gun is loaded and ready to fire. More kids are killed by accident from the shooting of an "empty" gun than are shot in the type of street violence glorified (and grossly exaggerated) in the movies. Even if you have some familiarity with guns, you must remember each weapon is different. Removing the clip from one gun might remove all the ammunition. Removing the clip from a similar but different gun might leave a bullet in the chamber.

Also, sometimes people do not realize how a gun works. For example, revolver owners sometimes check whether it is safe to pull the trigger by looking to see if there is a bullet in the cylinder positioned under the firing pin. They forget that the cylinder revolves. It is the bullet that is positioned to be the next in line for the firing pin that will be fired. The one you can see when checking the barrel will move to the next position as the trigger is pulled.

Some guns have safety catches to assure you cannot shoot them when you pull the trigger. However, not all safety catches work in the same way or need to be pushed in the same direction to be released so the gun can be fired.

The important point is that you cannot assume anything with a gun. Never point it at anyone. Never assume it is safe to pull the trigger.

Never touch the trigger until you are aiming at a target. Many law enforcement agencies train new police officers to draw their handguns with their fingers held stiffly down the side, next to the trigger. They move their finger over the trigger only when they are sighting on their target. Such a move takes a fraction of a second, but it assures the gun will not be accidentally fired. The same approach should be used with rifles and shotguns when carrying them.

2. Store guns properly.

The harder it is to get to a loaded gun and the longer it takes for you to be able to shoot, the safer it is. Ideally the gun should be unloaded and the ammunition stored in a separate, locked area.

A trigger lock should be used to reduce the chance of the gun being accidentally fired. Some manufacturers now provide trigger locks with every handgun they sell to improve safety. And

A firearms-safety-course instructor works with a teenage student.

some groups are taking legal actions to require manufacturers to outfit each gun with a trigger lock.

Bullets should be stored in a locked area away from the gun. The gun should be kept unloaded and uncocked in a gun vault or other unit designed to keep weapons secure. Some companies sell locking glass display cabinets, but these are easy to get into by breaking the glass. These are poor choices for safe storage.

If you are given the responsibility of cleaning a gun, be certain to learn the gun's proper care and storage. Then, before cleaning, check twice to see that it is unloaded. Do not handle the trigger except when necessary, and be certain the gun is pointing in a safe direction. Always clean the weapon alone to reduce the chance of accidentally hurting someone.

3. Educate yourself.

Anyone old enough to handle a gun kept in the home should take a firearms safety course. There are age-appropriate courses available from a variety of sources. The National Rifle Association can provide information about regional safety programs. Many gun stores have such information as well.

4. Recognize a gun at risk.

If your parents buy a gun for home protection, they may wish to keep the weapon near at hand. It may be kept on a nightstand or in the drawer of a table near the bed. It may be kept under a pillow or under a mattress so the person is able to reach it even before he or she moves out of bed.

This convenience carries risks and problems. First, children in the household may learn of the gun and want to see it. They may sneak into the bedroom to play with it. In one Florida incident, the mother of a teenager kept a loaded .38 in a bedroom nightstand. Her children knew about the gun and were told to leave it alone. The gun was always loaded and never had a trigger guard or other safety feature. When her teenage daughter was having trouble with her boyfriend, her schoolwork, and her part-time job, her mother got angry at her. They argued and the teenager said very hurtful things. When she calmed down, she was so ashamed that she wrote a note saying that her "big mouth" got her in trouble and it would be her "big mouth" that would end the pain. She then put the gun in her mouth and pulled the trigger. If there had not been a gun in the home, if she had not had access to a gun when she was so emotionally upset, it is possible that she would not have acted, or that someone could have helped her see beyond her immediate distress.

A second problem is that these guns are available to unsupervised children. In 1990, the *Journal of the American Medical Association* reported that more than 1.2-million latch-key children had access to guns in their homes. If anything, the figures have risen since then.

Equally important is the chance of theft. Parents would not have a gun unless they believed there were dangers. But they are not home every day, and burglars are aware of the most common places people keep guns when they own them for protection. Police departments say that burglars, like home owners, will go to the bedside stand, the mattress, the pillow, and the dresser drawers.

More secure measures should be taken. Except when everyone is sleeping, the gun should be inaccessible through a combination of trigger lock, putting the ammunition in a separate place, perhaps the removal of a critical part for firing, and the use of one or more gun safes (some gun owners use one gun safe to keep weapons and a second one to store ammunition). If a gun is in the house, only at the last minute before going to sleep should it be made reasonably accessible and ready for loading.

Having said this, it is important to question why a gun is ever in the house for protection. Nowhere in the United States have I seen crime statistics indicating families are in danger of being murdered in their beds. The rare kidnapping or murder in a home, such as happened to one child during a slumber party, is news because it is so extremely rare. Still, if a person feels the need for protection, a noisy burglar alarm connected by telephone to a central monitoring station provides a better safeguard. A companion dog that barks at strangers approaching the house provides better protection. And neither of these forms of protection will result in the accidental death of a loved one or neighbor.

5. If you see someone mishandling a weapon, call 911.

This is true if it is a family member, a friend, an acquaintance, or anyone else. In some communities, for example, it is popular to fire handguns and rifles into the air on the Fourth of July and New Year's. The shooters forget that the bullets

96

eventually come down, endangering anyone in their path. The gunfire puts everyone at risk, and the police will stop it.

6. Don't touch a strange weapon.

If you see a gun and think it might be real, tell an adult. Do not pick it up. Do not let others touch it if you can stop them. Leave and find an adult to help. If you don't know if it is real, assume it is.

7. If a friend's family keeps a gun and you feel that it is left in an unsafe manner, say something.

If the parents do not correct the problem, do not go to the friend's house. Asking your friend to always come to your home, or meet at a mall or somewhere else, may put a slight strain on the friendship, but a 1986 study by the *New England Journal of Medicine* found that guns kept in the home for self-protection are forty-three times more likely to kill someone the gun owner knows than to be used in self-defense. By 1997, the National Center For Health Statistics had found that fourteen American children are killed daily with guns.

8. There is never a good reason to take a gun to school.

Do not bring one and report anyone who has done so. The next chapter tells how to establish programs for this. The reasons someone might want to show off by bringing a gun to school are many, and most kids are not thinking of shooting it. But anything can happen with a handgun, and they have no place in a classroom show-and-tell.

9. Do not let someone who has a gun think you are impressed.

Some kids who carry guns want to intimidate or make you think they are special. The less attention you give them, the better. But do report it.

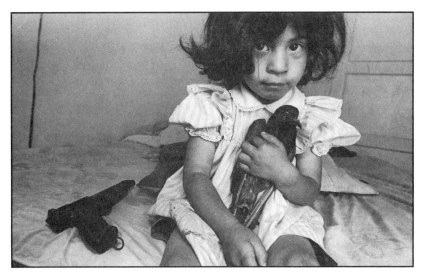

If guns are in the home, it is difficult to keep children from finding them. This three-year-old, holding a wounded pigeon, can load and fire the B-B gun, and also knows where her uncle's "real gun" is kept.

Chapter 8
What Can You Do to Keep Your School Safe?

Keeping your school safe from gun violence begins with you. Most adults think that violence is a threat for someone else's kids, someone else's school—unless the school has already experienced violence.

"We don't have gangs here," one principal will say. "Our students come from good homes and most are going on to college immediately after graduation." "Our kids aren't angry or depressed," another will say. "Look at our college board scores. Look at the way they support their athletic teams and their involvement with extracurricular activities." "Best time of their lives. Stop worrying and let them enjoy themselves," yet another will comment. "Wait until they get out in the real world. Then they'll know how lucky they are right now."

"Don't be a tattletale."

"I don't want you exaggerating."

"I don't want you telling a lie just to get attention."

"Yes, I'm sure you believe what you're saying, but I think you're overreacting to another kid's bragging."

"Are you trying to cause me trouble by making these wild accusations?"

These comments demonstrate the ostrich syndrome and many adults suffer from it.

You and your classmates are probably not any better. Most kids think they are immortal or will at least have very long lives. The idea of sudden death or serious injury is beyond their ability to imagine. You feel young, strong, with an exciting future ahead of you. Imagining yourself as a victim is impossible. You are as likely to think "it can't happen here" as your parents and teachers.

Except that in your heart you know better. You know the kids who are ridiculed. You know the kids who talk about violence, about suicide, about revenge. You know who is troubled. And you have a responsibility to break the code of silence.

Defining the Problem

Gangs are perhaps adults' greatest concern when they wonder if guns are in their children's school. And, gangs are even more common than most adults realize. They can be found among the rich and the poor, among whites as well as blacks, Asians, and Hispanics. A few years ago gangs were found in Rancho Santa Fe, California, at the time one of the richest communities in the nation. The parents were often top executives in entertainment and business. And their children were driven in luxury cars, enjoyed trips around the world, and were given expensive private school educations. Yet some of the children had formed gangs and were burglarizing each other's homes after sharing their parents' burglar alarm codes.

Gangs have always been a problem in schools. For many youths, the gang is partly a family, partly a test of adulthood, partly a way to rebel while being emotionally supported by others of a similar mind. The gang members frequently fight among themselves, fight rival gangs, and fight kids who have refused to join them.

In the past, weapons were makeshift to avoid detection. Often a single gun was brought to the site of a "rumble." It usually was a loaded revolver with five or six rounds of ammunition. One gang member would fire all the bullets at the rival gang, and then the two sides would fight with fists, knives, automobile antennas, chains, belts with heavy metal buckles, and other scrabbled-together weapons. Kids were hurt and sometimes killed, but that was still milder than what happens today in some gangs whose members maintain an arsenal of Mac-10's, Uzis, and other deadly weapons.

Sometimes the gangs are obvious to everyone. They deliberately wear their clothing in a manner that identifies their gang. This might mean wearing red or blue or some other color. This might mean wearing oversized pants hung low (the sagging and bagging of some urban gangs), or one pants leg rolled up while the other is left down.

This is not to say that all teens who dress in a conspicuously different way are gang members. Gang "chic" frequently becomes part of the teen culture. Hip-hop clothing and hairstyles, tattoos, branding, and the wearing of gang symbols are as likely to be found among upper-income, predominantly white non-gang-member teens as they are in the inner city.

There are times when a gang is well known to the students but not obvious to anyone else. Shaker Heights (Ohio) High School serves one of the most affluent suburban communities in the United States. The students are the children of doctors, lawyers, members of the Cleveland Orchestra, professors, and business leaders, among others. College board scores are invariably high, and the school runs a respected Advanced Placement (AP) program.

A few years ago, Shaker Heights High had a gang that was well known to many of the students, but unknown or ignored by the faculty. It was called the AP Posse. All the members of the AP Posse were extremely intelligent. Some hung out with their friends from advanced placement classes; some were also involved with music programs and other interests. What they shared was a desire to spend time together, engaging in activities ranging from casual sex to the drinking of large quantities of codeine-based cough syrup to, in one case, possible murder. There were periodic run-ins with law enforcement, but no one got in serious trouble because their parents were prominent and they looked like typical "good kids." Only their classmates were aware of the truth, and none of them felt they could discuss the matter with adults. Teachers and parents gave the impression that they did not want to know that the school's best and brightest students held the

In every high school, even in prosperous, safe communities, some students have guns.

potential for causing serious trouble. The adults were unprepared for violence. Just as they were unprepared in Pearl, Mississippi, until after Luke Woodham got a gun.

Gangs may be a bigger problem than schools outside the inner cities are willing to acknowledge, but a kid does not have to be a gang member to have a gun.

When a kid has access to a gun, there are many reasons why he or she may carry it to school. The most common reason kids give is fear of someone. This has been demonstrated in interviews conducted in schools throughout the United States. The fear might be of a bully whose taunting has, in the student's mind, gotten out of hand. This might be fear of or anger with a group of students who make fun of the student. It might be in response to a threat by a rival, such as in one school where a girl brought a gun because another girl had threatened, "I'll get my Daddy's gun and shoot you if you don't leave my boyfriend alone."

For some kids, carrying a gun is a way of getting attention. The gun is brought to show off to friends. This is not about fear. The student thinks that having the gun provides status, that other students will show him or her more respect. The student's gratification is like that of the first kid in class to get a superstar's signature sneakers.

The problem is more than guns, of course. The problem is with weapons, a gun being the most feared because a bullet can travel and affect innocents who may be so far away from the shooter that they don't hear the gunfire.

In 1994, the U.S. government maintained that one high school student in every five routinely carried a weapon to school. Such weapons include knives, razor blades, screwdrivers, and the like. They also included guns, with an estimated one student in twenty having a gun in class on any given day. This means that if you were to look around your high school classroom, no matter where you go to school, no matter how nice the kids might be, there is a good chance that one kid in every class has access to a gun that he or she has carried to school. Most say it is for self-defense against some real or imagined enemy. In Stamps, Arkansas, for example, on December 15, 1997, Joseph Todd, then fourteen, was arrested after shooting two classmates at random. According to the sheriff, Todd felt that he had been bullied by his classmates too often. He didn't care who he shot with the .22 rifle he brought from home. He just wanted to cause others pain.

So what can you do to reduce the problem and take back your school?

The Programs

Dr. N. Wesley Boughner, a retired Michigan school superintendent who has taught in schools around the world, fears that students alone can do little about the problem of weapons in school. He says that there must be adult recognition of the dangers. Too many teachers, principals, and parents refuse to admit that there might be a danger until something terrible happens. They ignore the students who are nervous about problems they know are festering. Thus the adults must recognize the truth and work together to end the problem.

Other school leaders stress that while there is little students can do without adult support, they can be initiators of the process that brings change. Your role, and it is critical, is to be willing to go to both adults and other kids in order to start the process to reduce the risk of violence. This means acquainting yourself with what can and should be done, something you are doing as you complete this book, and talking with trusted adults to encourage action.

"Talk with your guidance counselor," Dr. Boughner suggests. "Most kids trust their guidance counselor and know that what is said will be kept private. You can talk about problems you are seeing and should feel comfortable knowing what you say will not be told to others.

"Talk with a trusted teacher. And if other approaches don't work, go directly to either the principal or the assistant principal, whoever you feel will be most willing to talk with you." Dr. Boughner also suggests getting parents and clergy involved.

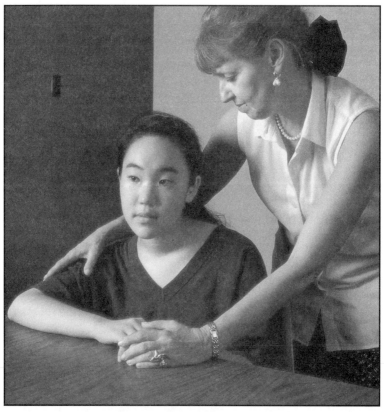

A troubled student can find understanding and help from a trusted counselor or other adult.

What types of programs can students, parents, and school faculties consider? One of the most successful programs in schools is the WARN Program of Reseda High School in California. Developed by Dr. Robert Kladifko and Dr. Jay Shaffer, the program was created after a shooting at the high school. One student brought a small caliber gun to class to shoot another student. This shocking event was made more distressing by the fact that seven students knew about the weapon before it was used. The seven were not trying to protect a friend when they maintained silence. They had no idea where to go, who to tell, and who would listen to them.

WARN stands for Weapons Are Removed Now. It is a partnership among students, teachers, school administrators, parents, and neighbors living and working around the school. The first step in the WARN program is to make the school a safe place for learning and being with classmates. At Reseda High School a uniformed police officer is always available to the students. The officers are chosen for their professionalism, friendliness, and belief in the right of all students to have an education free from fear. They work with the students to prevent problems, rather than seeing students as the enemy—an important distinction.

The campus has metal detectors at the school entrance doors, and a fence to restrict access. There are periodic random student searches, and other security measures. There is also a toll-free number posted in the school and around campus so students can report a weapon without identifying themselves. The program is completely anonymous, yet each tip is taken seriously. If anyone threatens violence, if anyone is spotted bringing a weapon to school or even talking about doing so, students, teachers, parents, and neighbors

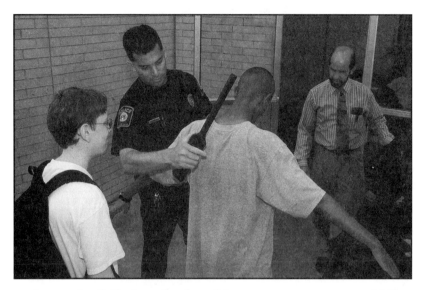

As part of their school safety programs, some middle schools and high schools require students to pass through a metal detector before entering school.

can use the toll-free number to tell what is happening. An investigation always follows, and if the story proves groundless, that is okay. If there is truth to the call, then it is handled appropriately.

One controversial element in Reseda's program is the random searches. At this writing they are still taking place, and some students approve of them. However, such searches have been declared illegal. Each school system must work within local and federal laws, as well as considering what students and parents think is fair. Can book bags be searched when entering the school? Book bags have been used to conceal weapons, yet they are a convenience for all students and few want to find another way to carry their supplies. Likewise, locker searches are questionable in the minds of some authorities, the question being whether the locker is school property or student property. These are issues for each school system to work through.

"I have what I call the Principal's Inner Ear Program," Dr. Kladifko says. "It's like my student cabinet. It includes forty natural leaders from all the grades so there are new people every year."

The "natural leaders" are a widely varied group of students. Reseda High School includes families of many cultures and backgrounds. There are thirty-five different languages spoken by the students, and the natural leaders include gang leaders and athletes. "The other students look up to them," said Dr. Kladifko, and as a result, when students feel uncomfortable talking with an adult, they can talk with one of the forty leaders. Equally important, the forty are trained in conflict resolution and peer mediation. They are often able to resolve a dispute before weapons are a consideration.

The idea of conflict resolution is important. One of the main reasons the issue of weapons arises in any school is because students do not know how to resolve their differences. You may have heard little kids, perhaps your own younger brother or sister, arguing on the playground. You may see an accident, for example. One kid running across the schoolyard, not looking where he is going, accidentally bumps into another kid. That kid, not realizing no harm was meant, decides that the first student deliberately knocked him over. Then the child who was running becomes angry because he is accused of something. But rather than discussing it, each is soon calling the other names, making threats, perhaps retaliating physically.

Or a child who has been teased over his or her race, hairstyle, clothing, or anything else, begins to feel defensive. The child looks for sinister motives in everything that happens. He or she becomes defensive,

Schools are using a variety of programs to reach young children. Here children in a Cease Fire anti-gun program turn in plastic guns.

always ready for a fight, until violence erupts over something as foolish as the way the child thinks a classmate is looking at him.

Learning better ways to handle differences is critical for children, including those in elementary school. Programs such as WARN offer this training, and also send trained high school students back to their elementary and middle schools to instruct the younger students.

"We get into groups and write skits, plays, songs, anything we think will get the message across," said WARN member Claudia De La Torre, a 1998 Reseda High graduate who has been active in everything from cheerleading to student politics. "We put on a show at the elementary schools and take WARN buttons and bumper stickers. The kids are going to the same schools we went to, and they look up to us. They listen when we try to tell them about changing their values about snitching."

"We show them they can get hurt if someone brings a gun to school. The bullet has no name on it. It can hit anyone when fired, not just the shooter's intended target. Telling on a friend is the best thing you can do. Otherwise you or a friend can get hurt. You can die," said WARN member Gabriela Lopez, the 1998 Reseda High School student body president. She explained that the students meet during their lunch hour to plan what they do. They also are evaluated by the kids in the schools where they put on skits. In that way they can find new and better ways to get the message across.

"We show them they have to break the code of silence," said Claudia De La Torre. "It's okay to tell."

And telling means telling about all problems. Dr. Kladifko spoke about one student who mentioned that another student seemed depressed. The school psychologist was notified and the boy contacted within ten minutes. The boy was potentially suicidal, but after counseling, he was able to stop thinking of violence and eventually returned to an active, happy school experience.

Sometimes it's only a few minutes in a student's life that can make a difference for everyone. It's finding a way to handle anger or learning another way to look at a problem. It's having someone listen to complaints, even if the person doesn't necessarily agree. The contacts must always be done anonymously so that no one fears retaliation or embarrassment.

The Reseda program also addresses one of Dr. Boughner's other concerns—involvement with the community. In addition to the toll-free number posted around the high school, Dr. Kladifko and other community leaders created KYDS—Keep Youth Doing Something. KYDS programs, coordinated with city officials and others, range from working for the Parks and Recreation Department to coed softball games. KYDS has sponsored career days, field trips, and other activities which offer opportunities to explore the future while becoming involved with adults from all parts of the community.

Many of these programs require adult leadership and coordination. Most are what might be called reactive—they will draw adult support after the schools are shown to be handling problems and potential problems, an area where you can be involved.

Another program that is working in locations where work schedules allow is "Security Dads." Fathers volunteer at their children's schools for whatever days they can. They wear T-shirts with the words "Security Dad" on it. Each father takes a turn at being at the school, usually with several other fathers. They act as additional security. They are familiar faces to the students, people they also will see when they are not in school. The students learn that the fathers care. They also realize that parents do talk with each other. And most importantly, they learn that their parents feel that school is important, that learning is important, and that they will give their time to assure that nothing interferes with their children getting an education.

What Can You Do at School?

There is a great deal of material available to help both adults and kids anxious to attack the problems in their schools. For full information, you can contact the following groups, which work with both students and adults. Remember that some require adults to initiate the action, but the adults cannot act if they do not know what is available. You can be the facilitator for change in your school.

The National School Safety Center, 4165 Thousand Oaks Blvd., Suite 290, Westdale Village, California

91362. This is a clearing house for information. It can guide you to appropriate programs for your school and community.

Child Safety Network (CSN), Adolescents Violence Prevention Resource Center, Educational Development Center Inc., 55 Chapel Street, Newton, Massachusetts 02158-1060. Again, this is a resource for a broad range of information.

The American Bar Association School Mediation Project, ABA Special Committee on Dispute Resolutions, 1800 M Street, NW, Washington, D.C. 20036. This is a program to help you learn how to handle conflicts in school. The program was developed and is managed by the largest national organization for lawyers.

The Quest Program is an excellent program to help you and your classmates develop ways to deal with conflict. It teaches everything from how little kids can learn to not overreact, to how teenagers can explore conflict issues and find ways to prevent violence. The program has a web site at www.quest.edu. This has become a major project for the Lions Club International. In many communities, it is only through the Lions Club support that schools can afford to implement the programs and training. Contact Lions Club International, Youth Programs Department, 300 22nd Street, Oak Brook, Illinois 60523-8842. As with the WARN program, there are QUEST programs for students in kindergarten through fifth grade, for students in sixth through eighth grades, and programs for high schools. Each is unique and appropriate for the concerns of the different age groups.

Syndistar, Inc., 5801 River Rd., New Orleans, Louisiana 70123-5106. This company made Reseda High School's WARN program available nationally. The

Fourth and fifth grade students in an anger management program serve as mediators to demonstrate non-violent ways to solve conflicts.

company offers videotapes and written materials on a variety of subjects of concern to students and teachers. The WARN tape is just eight minutes long but demonstrates the program through the eyes of the students involved. Another excellent tape specifically for kids is a two-part video that deals with alternatives to violence. It presents conflict resolution, negotiation, and mediation.

Recently many cities have explored conflict resolution and peer mediation programs. These allow students who have been specially trained to work with other students to settle problems. There may be a mediation panel of students as well. However, in communities lacking such programs, as well as in those where a supplement would be helpful, the Syndistar program is excellent.

Other Syndistar videos and materials are for adults and address issues such as identifying suicidal and at-risk youth and the prevention of violence through analysis of the school. The latter deals with all aspects of school safety including preventing people who wish to inappropriately use or harm students from getting access to schools. The costs vary and preview materials are available from the company. They are especially helpful for school districts where there are no area programs, and budget limitations prevent the hiring of outside experts.

Finally, if you do your best to help friends and classmates and to promote safety awareness in your school and something still happens, do not feel you are at fault. Kyle Foster, who was finishing his junior year at Pearl High School when Luke Woodham got his gun, later questioned whether he could have done more to head off the shooting. "I've known Luke since second grade," Kyle told me. "We took a lot of classes together. Maybe if I had brought him in with my friends, he wouldn't have done what he did."

The truth is that kids tend to come together based on shared interests. Kyle is an athlete, physically active. He is bright, but the practice sessions for the sports he enjoys take up much of his free time. Luke was involved with a different group of kids. He had no interest in sports and was not likely to be friendly with Kyle. Certainly he had never told Kyle of his feelings about being picked on. He never talked about his rage. He never threatened to get a weapon when Kyle was around to hear such comments. It would have been difficult for Kyle to have known there was a problem, much less to have tried to head it off.

The same is true for you. You can do your part to protect your home, family, and school from weapons.

Thousands of kids are killed or badly hurt

by

guns every year

Now, they can't play sports...

can't drive...

can't dance...

can't even walk, talk or see.

These are the kids who lived!

But the problem requires kids and adults working together. It requires recognizing that no single person, no matter how dedicated, can do it all. Violence has happened in the past and it will happen again. There is much you can do to reduce the chance it will happen in your school, but ultimately all of us have to work together. And even then, something can happen that could not have been avoided.

You hope you will not be a part of one of the tragedies that have affected a number of schools. You hope your efforts, along with those of your classmates, teachers, administrators, and parents, will head off trouble before it occurs. But if the worst should happen, know that you did your best and you are not responsible. This is a problem all of us will be dealing for many years to come.

What Can You Do with Friends and Acquaintances?

There is a myth that if someone talks about doing harm to his or her self or others, the person will not act. In truth, most kids who are having problems talk about them. They express their anger, depression, frustration. In many cases, they are talking before they act. But they are talking because they are seriously considering acting and probably will. The psychologists interviewed for this book agree on the following points:

If someone wants to talk with you about depression, suicide, or acting out violently, listen. Do not be judgmental. Do not say the person should not do it. Just listen and let him or her express the feelings.

If the person will listen, suggest that there might be another way to handle the problem. Mention an appropriate teacher, clergy member, or other adult if you know one the person trusts. If not, after you have left the person, ask an adult you trust to help.

If the person shows you a gun or other weapon, report it as soon as possible. However, do not react with shock, horror, excitement, or statements such as, "That's crazy. Put it away before someone gets hurt." At that moment the person probably does want someone to hurt.

Alcohol, marijuana, and other drugs will increase any problem. They may lower inhibitions, increase depression, or otherwise alter the ability to think clearly.

If one adult will not take your concerns seriously, go to someone else. You must not give up when you know a problem exists.

Remember that if you have a friend who is emotionally disturbed and considering violence, the person may not be disturbed for life. Once a potentially violent action has been stopped, once the person has had appropriate therapy, what you saw and liked in that friend is still there. Don't shun other kids who went through bad times once those bad times are over.

Chapter **9**

Points to Remember

About School Safety

Everyone has the right to go to school without fear of violence.

There is never a good reason to have a weapon in school.

Kids get hurt, crippled, and killed by guns in school. You may not be the target of the person doing the shooting. Most of the kids hurt in recent school shootings were not intended targets.

You must break the code of silence when you know or have reason to think that someone is going to hurt his or her self or others. If your school has no way to report the matter anonymously, talk with a trusted counselor, teacher, or other adult. If you feel the matter is not being taken seriously, go to a different person, the principal, or anyone you think will take you seriously.

Kids talk about tattletales, snitches, squealers, finks, rats, and the like. The names hurt. But there is a difference between complaining about a fellow kindergartner who sneaks crayons from other kids and a kid talking about or carrying a weapon. The code of silence can get you or your best friend killed.

SAFETY PLEDGE

If I see a gun or anything that looks like a gun

I will not touch it,

I will go get an adult,

Because guns can hurt me

And I want to be safe.

IT'S NOT COOL
TO FOOL WITH GUNS

About Gun Safety

- Never handle a loaded gun.
- All guns are loaded.
- When you see a gun where it should not be, leave and get an adult.

- Do not react if a classmate shows you a gun. When you are away from the person, report what has happened.
- Guns are safer when stored in a way that makes them harder to use. A trigger lock is a help. Storing the ammunition and the weapons in separate, locked holders meant to secure them should be routine. Remove the firing pin when cleaning so that the gun has to be reassembled before use.
- If a gun is kept for protection, it should be locked away whenever the adult responsible for its use is not at home.
- Plan a gun safety drill. If your parents keep a loaded gun near their bed at night, how can you safely get their attention if you need them? If you come rushing into their room, how will you avoid being accidentally shot? Plan for the worst possible event that led your parents to have a weapon, then decide how to avoid anyone getting hurt, even if that means not leaving the gun in a convenient place.
- As soon as they are old enough to be involved in such a program, every member of your family should take a course in gun handling, gun safety, and basic shooting. These are offered through the NRA, many gun shops, and gun clubs. See "For Further Information" at the end of this book.
- If you know that someone is mishandling a weapon, tell an adult. And if there is an accident, dial 911 to report it.

Remember that guns are only one type of weapon. All weapons can hurt or kill. All weapons should be treated with respect and extreme caution.

Buying a Gun

If your family is considering buying a gun for home protection, contact the organizations listed in the appendix for information for and against such ownership.

Talk about the dangers of having a gun, especially if there are small children in the home or if someone in your family is suffering from depression or irrational mood swings.

Tell your parents you do not want them to buy a gun unless they first take a course in gun safety.

And always remember that a weapon in the house is more of a danger for family members than for those who might wish to do you harm. Plan carefully so that you and your loved ones can avoid becoming statistics.

And Always . . .

Break the code of silence. Your concerns, expressed openly to adults who can intervene, may save many lives.

Notes

Chapter 1:

1. Information about Pearl, Mississippi, from the *Jackson Clarion-Ledger*, October 2, 1997; October 3, 1997; October 4, 1997. *People*, November 3, 1997. Author interviews in Pearl and by mail with Luke Woodham.

2. *Time*, April 6, 1998; July 6, 1998. *Cleveland Plain Dealer*, December 2, 1997; *New York Times*, December 2 and 3, 1997.

3. *Time*, April 6, 1998.

Chapter 2:

1. Michael Newton, *Armed and Dangerous: A Writer's Guide to Weapons* (Cincinnati: Writer's Digest Books, 1990).

2. James D. Horan, *The Authentic Wild West: The Outlaws* (New York: Crown, 1977).

3. Newton.

4. Author interview.

5. Louis Garavaglia and Charles Worman, *Firearms of the American West, 1803-1865* (Albuquerque: University of New Mexico Press, 1985).

6. Don B. Kates, Jr., *Restricting Handguns: The Liberal Skeptics Speak Out* (Barrington, Massachusetts: North River Press, 1979), p. 11.

7. Author interview.

8. Author interview.

Chapter 3:

1. Statistics compiled by the Center to Prevent Handgun Violence, 1225 I Street, N.W., Suite 1100, Washington, D.C., 20005.

Chapter 4:

1. Ibid.

2. Ibid.

3. Ted Schwarz, *Protect Your Home and Family* (New York: Arco Publishing, 1983).

Chapter 6:

1. Jack Gould, "Surrender to Television?," *New York Times*, June 16, 1968.

2. "TV on Trial," *Newsweek*, September 12, 1977, p. 104.

3. House Committee on Energy and Commerce, *Violence On Television*, Hearing before the Subcommittee On Telecommunications and Finance, 103rd Congress, Second Session, 1993.

4. Tonya Flynt-Vega and Ted Schwarz, *Hustled: My Journey from Fear to Faith* (Louisville, Kentucky: Westminster/John Knox Press, 1977). Also personal interviews with subject.

5. Interview with Dr. Kappas.

6. Interviews with Dr. Griffis.

7. Ibid.

8. Interview in Los Angeles.

For Further Information

Organizations

Campaign to Prevent Handgun Violence against Kids; 454 Las Gallinas Avenue, Suite 177, San Rafael, California 94903-3618

Center for Gun Policy and Research; Johns Hopkins School of Hygiene and Public Health, 624 N. Broadway, Baltimore, Maryland 21205-1996

Center to Prevent Handgun Violence; 1225 I Street, N.W., Suite 1100, Washington, D.C. 20036

Coalition to Stop Gun Violence; 1000 Sixteenth Street, N.W., Suite 603, Washington, D.C, 20036

Educational Fund to End Handgun Violence; 1000 Sixteenth Street, N.W., Suite 603, Washington, D.C. 20036

Gun Owners of America, Inc., 8001 Forbes Place, Suite 102, Springfield, Virginia 22151

Handgun Control, Inc., 1225 I Street, N.W., Suite 1100, Washington, D.C. 20005

National Rifle Association of America, 11250 Waples Mill Road, Fairfax, Virginia 22030

Books

Apel, Loreleia, *Dealing with Firearms at School and at Home*. New York: Rosen, 1996.

Gottfried, Ted, *Gun Control: Public Safety and the Right to Bear Arms*. Brookfield, CT: Millbrook, 1993.

Kleck, Gary, and Don Kates, *The Great American Gun Debate: Essays on Firearms & Violence*. San Francisco: Pacific Research for Public Policy, 1997.

Kopel, David B., ed. *Guns: Who Should Have Them?* Amherst, NY: Prometheus Books, 1995.

Krushke, Earl R. *Gun Control: A Reference Handbook*. Santa Barbara: ABS-CLIO, 1995.

Landau, Elaine. *Armed America: The Status of Gun Control*. Englewood Cliffs: Messner, 1991.

McGuckin, Frank, ed. *Violence in American Society*. New York: H.W. Wilson Co., 1998.

Schleifer, Jay. *Everything You Need to Know about Weapons in School and at Home*. New York: Rosen, 1994.

Spitzer, Robert J. *The Politics of Gun Control*. New York: Chatham House, 1998.

Internet Resources

Bureau of Alcohol, Tobacco and Firearms' Website:
http://www.atf.treas.gov/
Includes Youth Crime Gun Interdiction Initiative.

California Wellness Foundation Funds the Campaign to Prevent Handgun Violence Against Kids:
http://www.pcvp.org/firearms/other/policy3.html

Center to Prevent Handgun Violence:
http://www.handguncontrol.org/helping/

National Criminal Justice Information Center:
http://www.ncjrs.org/

National Rifle Association of America:
http://www.nra.org/

Student Pledge Against Gun Violence:
http://www.pledge.org/

Index

Gore, Tipper, 77
Griffis, Dale, 81-82, 84, 85
Gun control, 34-41, *39*
Gun show, *35*, 48-51, *49*, *50*

Hamilton, Alexander, 32
Herring, Paige Ann, 11
Hickock, Wild Bill, 16
Hinckley, John, 35, 36
History of guns, 12-21, *13*, *20*
Holt, Chauncey, 18
Home protection, 23-24, *23*,
    43, 46-47, 48, 94-96, 121
Hunting/sport, 14, 17-19,
    38, 39-40, 83
Hwika, John, 28

Internet, 83-85, 125

James, Jesse, 14
Johnson, Mitchell, 10-11,
    10, 52

Kappas, John, 77-79
Kinkel, Kipland, 53-54, *54*
Kladifko, Robert, 106, 108, 110

Lee, Richard Henry, 32
Levin, Gerald M., 80
Licensing of handguns, 35
Locker searches, 107-108
Lopez, Gabriela, 110

Makeshift weapons, 60, 101
Madison, James, 32
Masterson, Bat, 15
McCartney, Paul, 78
Menefee, Christina, 5

Mighty Morphin Power
    Rangers, 67
Militia, 31-34, *33*
Movies, 6-7, 7, 14, 22, 57, *58*,
    67. *See also* Television
Music, 77-80

National Guard, 31, 34, 53-54
National Rifle Association,
    35, 42-43, 94
Noam, Gil, 72

Obtaining guns, 48-53, *49*,
    50, 88-89
Organizations, 124

Plato, 72-73
Private ownership of guns,
    22, 43. *See also* Second
    Amendment

Radcliff, Jim, 27
Reagan, Ronald, 35, 36
Registering guns, 37-38, 51
Reiser, Martin, 69-70
Renting guns, 52
Right to bear arms. *See*
    Second Amendment
Rite of passage, 85-86
Role-playing games, 81-83

Safety, 44-48, *45*, 53-54,
    91- 98, *93*, *98*, 119-121
Saturday night specials, 36,
    48, 49
Schools, 41, 60, 83-84, 97,
    99-104, 111-117, *113*
    active groups, 111-112